THE DRAGON PRINCE OF ALASKA

ROYAL DRAGONS OF ALASKA
BOOK ONE

ELVA BIRCH

Copyright © 2020 by Elva Birch

All rights reserved.

ROYAL DRAGONS OF ALASKA

This book is part of the Royal Dragons of Alaska series. All of my work stands alone (always a satisfying happy ever after and no cliffhangers!) but there is a story arc across books. This is the order the series may be most enjoyed:

> The Dragon Prince of Alaska (Book 1)
> The Dragon Prince's Librarian (Book 2)
> The Dragon Prince's Bride (Book 3)
> The Dragon Prince's Secret (Book 4)
> The Dragon Prince's Magic (Book 5)

Subscribe to Elva Birch's mailing list and join her in her Reader's Retreat at Facebook for sneak previews!

CHAPTER 1

Carina Andresen surged to her feet, sweeping her camp chair out from under her as a make-shift weapon.

Wolf! her brain hammered at her. *Wolf!* She was going to become an Alaska tourist statistic and get eaten by a wolf on her second week in the kingdom.

Logic slowly caught up with her panic.

The animal across the campfire from her was smaller and *doggier* than a wolf, and it was only a moment before Carina could get her breath and heartbeat back under control and recognize that it was well-groomed, shyly eyeing her sizzling hot dog, and wagging its tail.

Alaska probably had stray dogs, too; she wasn't *that* far from civilization.

"Hi there, sweetie," Carina said, her voice still unnaturally high as she put her chair back on its legs. "Does that smell good? Want a bit of hot dog?" Carina turned the hot dog in the flame and waggled it suggestively.

The non-edible dog sped up his tail and when Carina broke off a piece of the meat and dropped it beside her, he crept around the fire and slurped it eagerly up off the ground.

The second bite he took gently from her fingers, and by the second hot dog she dared to pet him.

Within about thirty minutes and five hot dogs, he was leaning on her and letting her scratch his ears and neck as he wagged his tail and groaned in delight.

"Oh, you're just a dear," Carina said. "I bet someone's missing you." He was a husky mix, Carina guessed; he was tall and strong, with a long, thick coat of dark gray fur and white feet. His ears were upright, and his tail was long and feathered. He didn't have a collar, but he was clearly friendly. "You want some water?"

The dog licked his lips as if he had understood, and Carina carefully stood so she didn't frighten him.

But he seemed to be past any shyness now, and he followed Carina to her van trustingly, tail waving happily. He drank the offered water from a frying pan, and then tried to give Carina a kiss dripping with slobber.

"You probably already have a name," Carina said, laughingly trying to escape the wet tongue. "But I'm going to call you Shadow for now." She had a grubby towel hanging from her clothesline and used it to dry off his face. They played a gentle game of tug-of-war, testing each other's strength and manners.

Shadow seemed to approve of his new name and gave her a canine grin once she'd won the towel back from him.

"Alright, Shadow, let's go collect some more firewood."

The area was rich with downed wood to harvest, and with the assistance of a folding hand saw, Carina was able to find several heaping armloads of solid, dry wood, enough to keep a cheerful fire going for a few days if she was frugal. It was comforting to have Shadow around for the task; she wasn't quite as nervous about the noises she heard, and he was a happy distraction from her own brain.

He frolicked with her, and found a stick three times his own length to drag around possessively.

"So helpful!" Carina laughed at him, as he knocked over an empty pot and swiped her across the knees so that she nearly fell.

When she sat down beside the crackling fire in her low camp chair, Shadow abandoned his prize stick and crowded close to lay his head on her knee. Carina petted him absently.

"Someone's looking for you, you big softy," she said regretfully. She would have to try to reunite the dog with his owner but, for now, it was nice having a companion around the camp.

Of all the things she expected when she went running for the wilderness, she had never guessed that the silence would be the worst. She had been camping plenty, but it was always *with* someone. Since their parents had died, that someone was usually her sister, June, but sometimes it was a friend or a roommate. She was used to having someone to point out birds and animals to, someone to share chores with, stretch out tarps with. When it was just her, the spaces seemed vaster, the wind bit harder, and even the birds were less cheerful.

"You probably don't care about the birds that would make my life list," she told Shadow mournfully.

Shadow wagged his tail in a rustle of leaves.

She didn't have her life list anymore to add to anyway. Everything had been left behind: her phone, her computer, her identity. Her entire life was on hold. She had the van to live in, some supplies and a small nest egg to start from, so she ought to be able to stay out of sight long enough to regroup and…she didn't know what to do from here. Find a journalist willing to take her story and clear her name?

To fill the quiet, and to help ignore the ache in her chest, she read aloud from the brochure on Alaska that she had been given at the border station. She'd found it that evening while she was emptying the glovebox to take stock of supplies, and Shadow seemed as good a listener as any.

"Like many modern monarchies, Alaska has an elected council of officials who do most of the day to day rulings of this vast, rich land. The royal family is steeped in tradition and mystery, and holds many veto powers, as well as acting as ambassadors to other countries. Known as the Dragon King, the Alaskan sovereign is a reserved figure who rarely appears in public. Margaret, the Queen of Alaska, died twelve years ago, leaving behind six sons." There was a photo, with boys ranging from about seven to maybe twenty-five. Two of the middle children were identical. One of the twins was wearing a hockey jersey and grinning, the other wore glasses and looked annoyed. The oldest—or at least the tallest—was frowning seriously at the others. The only blonde of the bunch was one of the middle boys, who was looking intently at the camera. The youngest looked painfully bored. They all had tongue-twisting names of more syllables than Carina wanted to try pronouncing.

Carina thought it was an interesting photo. The tension between the oldest two was palpable, and they were all dressed surprisingly casually. She didn't follow royal gossip much beyond scanning headlines at grocery store checkouts, but Alaska never seemed to make waves; they were rarely involved in dramas and scandals.

Shadow raised his head and cocked his head at some imagined noise in the forest.

"That's a lot of siblings," Carina observed, ruffling his ears. She felt so much safer having him beside her. "Just one sister was more than enough for me." She didn't want to admit how much she missed that sister right now.

Shadow returned his head to her knee. "Alaska is a member of the Small Kingdoms Alliance, an exclusive collective of independent monarchies scattered throughout the world. Although Alaska has large amounts of land, they qualify for membership because of their small population."

Carina turned the brochure over. "There are hot springs about fifty miles north of Fairbanks! I hope to make it there." *Before* she ran out of cash. It looked expensive. Maybe she could get work there...she'd heard that it wasn't hard to find under-the-table jobs in this country.

Shadow suddenly leapt to his feet, barking at something crashing through the woods behind them and Carina nearly tipped over backwards in her camp chair trying to stand up.

She expected to find a moose, or possibly a bear, and she was already picking up the chair to use as a flimsy defense against a charging wild animal.

But it was only a man stepping out of the woods, in an official dark blue uniform emblazoned with the eight gold stars of Alaska.

For a moment, terror every bit as keen as the panic that had gripped her at the first sight of Shadow washed over her. They'd found her.

"You're trespassing on royal land and I'm going to have to ask you to leave," he said.

She realized with relief that it wasn't a police officer. He was only a park ranger.

CHAPTER 2

Toren could not understand his dragon's laser focus on their task. He was just rousting a squatter. They got a few colorful characters every year, usually in tents or old trucks, camping in the fringes of the royal forest. Once, one of the interlopers had managed to get a stolen train car hauled up an old logging road. Toren had helped Kenth carry the thing back to the rail yard, swearing the whole way.

He circled over the place—a break in the trees by a little stream with birch trees shaking down golden coins of leaves. There was a van pulled up to one side, one of the old style VW camper vans with the top that popped up. The squatter had obviously been there for some time; there was a blue tarp covering an area by the fire, and laundry was drying on lines strung between trees. There was a substantial pile of scavenged firewood, and an axe and handsaw lay nearby with a pair of gloves.

There, his dragon urged, as if Toren was incapable of noticing the figure sitting by a crackling fire with a gray dog.

I see him, Toren said.

Her, his dragon corrected avidly.

Toren looked for a place nearby to land and shift. If he could get the squatter to leave without revealing his dragon, he was supposed to do that, but he had some leeway; dragons —all shifters—were secret, but the type of person to trespass on royal lands was rarely the type to be taken seriously if they were raving about flying monsters.

It was a narrow clearing, mostly taken up by the dirty white van, so branches broke as Toren landed behind it, and he shifted swiftly, just as the dog barked in alarm and the woman—*Yes, her!*—rose from her fireside chair and turned.

Something washed over him—terror, he thought—and he realized that it was *her* terror. He felt like he'd just been drenched in cold water.

Make her feel better! Fix this! his dragon demanded.

Toren said the only words he could form, the ones he'd been practicing on his flight here: "You're trespassing on royal land and I'm going to have to ask you to leave."

For a moment, Toren had a bad feeling that she was going to fight him, her chair held in two grim hands and her dog growling at her side, then she laughed in giddy relief and lowered it.

"I know I'm not supposed to be here," she said sheepishly. "It was just such a nice place, and...um...the campground was full?" She was a terrible liar, blushing and full of hesitation, and Toren knew that tourist season was already ebbing. "If I promise to leave tomorrow, can I at least stay overnight and pack up in the morning?"

Toren would have agreed to anything she asked, would have handed over his entire hoard at the very hint of her desire for it. He felt like he was looking straight into her, straight at his own destiny, and he could feel all of her courage and all of her aching vulnerability. He had never been so swept away, like he was feeling too many emotions to fit in just this moment, like he was being flooded by a lifetime of them.

She was American, by her accent, and had been camping for some time by her smoky scent and messy braided hair. She was also, unwashed state or not, the most gorgeous woman that Toren had ever laid eyes on. Her face was red-cheeked and round, and the hopeful smile she was shining at him was utterly enchanting. Her sun-streaked blonde hair was escaping around her face like a golden halo. and her eyes were a hazel green that made Toren think of autumn moss and…kissing.

Everything about her made him think of kissing.

"You're on royal land," he repeated faintly.

"Do you really have to kick me out before dinner, though?" she asked winningly. He could somehow *feel* the almost hysterical relief off of her in waves. "I fed Shadow the rest of my hot dogs, but I have a can of chicken and a box of macaroni and cheese. The good kind of mac and cheese, with the squeeze cheese, and it makes way too much for me to eat by myself."

"You're inviting me to dinner?" Toren asked, dazzled.

Accept her offer, his dragon hissed at him. *Accept anything she offers us!*

"That's not something illegal here is it?' The woman's smile hesitated and Toren was sideswiped by her spike of fear. "I'm not trying to…er…bribe you or anything. Exactly. I just…" she looked down at her hands. "Never mind."

"No, nothing like that, nothing illegal," Toren assured her in a blind panic. "I'd… I'd like that!"

"I'm Carina," she said, setting her camp chair back down. "Have a, ah…" she looked around. "Let me get you a chair. Do you mind putting a log on the fire?"

Carina. It was the most beautiful name that Toren had ever heard. "Sure."

"I promise it's all deadwood, I didn't chop down any royal trees," she teased. "Or shoot any royal moose!"

She went around the back of the van and Toren picked up a few pieces of wood from the pile by the campfire and tossed them onto the flame.

The fire promptly went out.

"Oh, no," Toren said in a panic. "What have I done?" He poked at it futilely and all it did was smoke and sputter. The dog wagged his tail in clear amusement.

Just as Toren wondered if he had time to shift into his dragon form and light it on fire decisively, Carina returned with a second, mismatched camp chair, folded tight in a roll.

"What did you do to my fire?" she asked in horror.

"I, er, added wood?"

"You smothered the poor thing!" Carina said, shaking her head. She knelt and skillfully separated the logs, coaxing reluctant flame back to life. "You have to give it air, you know."

"I'm Toren," he managed to tell her, taking the chair as she stood back up. Her dog was sniffing his leg curiously and Toren cautiously patted his head before he tried to figure out which parts of the chair were which.

She watched him try unsuccessfully to set it up for a moment before she took the folded fabric and metal tubes back from him, unsnapped a strap, grasped two of the limbs, and magically set it down as an actual chair.

Toren sat gingerly into it. "Thanks." He almost tipped over backwards as the gray dog stuck its nose into his side. "I like your dog."

"He's not mine," she said swiftly, though she felt almost possessive to Toren's addled senses. "He just showed up a

THE DRAGON PRINCE OF ALASKA

little while ago. He likes hot dogs, and I'm calling him Shadow."

"He seems friendly." Toren said, patting him absently. "No collar?" He was still having trouble thinking around the dazzling presence of Carina, who was busily fussing with the fire and balancing a grate over the flames between two piles of rocks.

"Nope," Carina said. "I should take him to Fairbanks and have him checked for a chip."

"Will you keep him?" Toren asked. "If he doesn't have an owner?"

"I'd like to," Carina said, kneeling beside him to rub Shadow's ears. "But I didn't really budget for dog food. And look how well cared for he is! Someone is bound to be looking for him."

Toren could hear the longing in her voice. She'd already lost her heart to the canine and Toren was unfairly jealous.

"Do you really live here?" he had to ask. "In that van?"

"Well, I did," Carina said plaintively. "But apparently I'm on royal land."

Toren wanted to drown in those eyes. How could he explain that he wanted her to stay with him...not just for a day or a week, but for a lifetime. *Why do I feel like I've been hit on the head?* he demanded of his dragon.

Our mate, his dragon sighed, and Toren really did fall out of his rickety camp chair then, startling so hard that he grabbed the arm and managed to half-fold it around himself as Shadow dashed back with a yelp of alarm before he toppled backwards.

Carina's laughter was like sunshine as she reached to help him up. "I should have warned you about the chair," she said kindly, and then her hand was in Toren's, and something inside him clicked.

He'd never expected true love, and it had honestly never

occurred to him before that the Compact might tap *him* to be king. But now, nothing could be more right, or more perfect, because Carina *was* his mate, and he recognized her, who she was, and everything they could be together.

And then he remembered what else that meant.

CHAPTER 3

Carina pulled Toren easily to his feet and then stood too close to him for a moment before she could get her raging hormones under control. He was the most gorgeous man she'd ever seen, and it seemed like it had been a long time since she'd been this close to one.

He was tall and strong, with a grin frozen on his face that showed straight, white teeth. He had dark hair and light eyes that were probably blue but looked almost silver in the evening light. He had a fresh, clean-shaven look that was either youth or really good personal grooming, and he smelled like night sky and stone, with a weird after-scent of sulfur. She kept thinking that his face must be really expressive, because she could read his confusion like a book, but really, he was mostly just grinning like some kind of sports model who'd just won a competition he hadn't entered.

"Thanks," he breathed.

"First time in a camp chair?" Carina teased, finally remembering to let go of him. "I'm guessing you haven't been a park ranger long."

"No," he said. "Not long. Brand new. To all of this."

His clothing certainly did look new, and Carina thought with appreciation that the flattering lines of the Alaska ranger garb was a lot better than either the American or the Canadian version. She'd always been a sucker for a guy in a uniform, but this was something more. The stars looked like real gold, and the detail in the stitching...made her realize that she was still standing entirely too close. She seemed to be swirling in emotions, and none of them really made sense. Some of them didn't even seem to be *hers*, and that was just crazy.

"Anyway, I'm sorry about the chair," Carina said apologetically, stepping back. "I don't use it and didn't realize what a piece of crap it is." She set it back up again, noting that one of the arms was considerably more bent than it had been.

"You live here *alone?*" Toren eyed the chair in challenge and once again lowered himself into it.

"It's the twenty-first century. Women do that all the time nowadays." Carina tamped down her flash of fear. He was just asking an innocent question. He probably wasn't thinking that it seemed *suspicious.*

He blushed. "I meant no offense, I only...ah..."

The wind chose that moment to shift, and they got faces full of thick smoke. Carina coughed and moved, only to have the smoke follow her. "It knows," she said, waving ineffectively in front of her face as her eyes stung from the irritation. "Oh, the water is ready!"

"Can I help?" Toren threatened to tip over his camp chair trying to stand up. The smoke didn't seem to bother *him* at all.

"No, sit! I got this. There's only room for one camp cook."

He subsided.

The pot she'd put over the fire was starting to boil, and she opened the macaroni and cheese box and dumped in the noodles. She popped the top off of the canned chicken and

THE DRAGON PRINCE OF ALASKA

drained it into the hottest part of the fire, then set it to the side of the grate to warm.

"You...ah...seem really good at this." Toren seemed to have the hang of his camp chair at last and was at least no longer tipping one direction and then another.

Carina reminded herself that it was an innocent question, not an interrogation. "Yeah," she said cautiously. "I went camping a lot as a kid. Things sort of went sideways with my life and Alaska seemed like the kind of place I could...get away for awhile."

To her surprise, he didn't follow that with questions, and Carina was glad she didn't have to tell him any lies. She was terrible at lying.

"So what do you do? When you aren't being kind of hopeless at rangering?"

Toren grinned at her again, and Carina felt her heart give a dangerous skip.

"I play hockey, go hunting. I like...ah...flying?"

Carina laughed. "You really are the cliché of an Alaskan. Even if your campfire skills do leave a lot to be desired."

She was beginning to doubt he really was a ranger, even a brand spanking new one. There wasn't any other real reason for a strange guy in an official Alaska uniform to be wandering around in the forest, but Carina didn't want to pry. And as long as it wasn't an official Alaska *police officer* uniform, she didn't really care what he was; if he wasn't going to enforce his move-out orders, she was going to stay as long as she possibly could.

Mostly because she had no idea what to do next.

She stirred the noodles and tasted one, burning her fingertips as she spooned it out of the bubbling water. "Ouch, ouch. Needs another minute."

She took that time to go to the van and dig out a second

bowl and spoon. Then she considered, and got a third bowl. On her way back, she paused to stare at her visitors.

Toren was sitting in a plume of smoke, completely oblivious to it, murmuring at Shadow as he stroked his ears. The canine was leaning his head into the man's lap, his fluffy tail thumping in the dirt.

In the space of about an hour, she had somehow acquired a guy and a dog...and Carina was disturbed by how comfortable it felt. She liked the idea of sharing her food, of having someone to make observations to, of having someone to warm her cold bed...

Carina shook her head firmly. She had problems to solve, problems that didn't involve roping anyone else into her mess, and if she stood here daydreaming like a schoolgirl, her next problem was going to be a mass of overcooked noodles she couldn't serve anyone. Even the dog would turn up his nose.

She drained the noodles and stirred in the cheese packet and canned chicken more vigorously than strictly necessary. "Dinner is served," she said, setting a small bowl in front of Shadow, who wolfed it down like she hadn't just fed him all her hot dogs. "A spoon for the park ranger with opposable thumbs," she said, handing Toren the utensil and a heaping bowl of food.

She settled into her own camp chair and tried not to watch Toren too obviously. He took the bowl with a polite murmur of thanks, but his look was clearly skeptical. It was a rather unattractive color and texture and Carina suspected that he was used to better fare by his careful manners and hesitant taste.

But campfire smoke had a near-magic way of making everything taste better than it otherwise should, and Toren's face lit up with delight. "This is great," he said, eating enthusiastically.

Carina was surprised to burn her tongue on her first bite, given the way both Shadow and Toren had downed theirs without hesitation. "One of my favorite meals," she said, sucking air into her mouth to cool it. "Not that classy, maybe, but always delicious."

It was crazy, how sexy he managed to look, eating fluorescent food from a chipped plastic bowl with a bent spoon. He had clearly mastered the camp chair, perched with his weight carefully balanced on the rickety structure. Carina couldn't stop watching the way his shoulders moved, and the way the evening light fell on his cheekbones. He was utterly gorgeous, and she had never been so immediately attracted to someone in her life.

She had to wrench her eyes away and focus on her food. She had bigger things to worry about.

He finished first, and Shadow came to beg at her feet as she polished off her last few bites. "You got yours," she scolded him. "*And* all my hot dogs."

He twitched his ears down and wagged his tail eagerly.

She let him lick out her bowl, and then the pot she'd stirred the food in, and she and Toren shared a giggle as he had to chase it around until he could corner it against the foot of Toren's chair, nearly unseating him again.

"Can I get you a drink?" she offered, when she stood to collect the dishes. "I've got water, I think there's a beer left, tea, instant coffee."

"Thank you, no. May I help you…in some fashion?" Park ranger or not, he had beautiful manners, Carina thought. Not the kind of kiss-up manners of someone who wanted something, just casual, well-bred polish. Maybe it was just how Alaskans were. Carina had been expecting more surliness and rough edges.

"Thanks, no. I've got a system." Carina rinsed the dishes

in the stream and set the pot full of stream water on the grate. She wouldn't drink it, but it was fine for washing up.

The sun was just down behind the mountains, slowly sinking, and the sky overhead was purple and streaked with red and orange clouds. The falling birch leaves made a soothing whisper just audible above the babbling of the little stream, and it smelled like campfire smoke and moss.

"This is my favorite time of day, and my favorite time of year," Carina said contentedly, for the rare moment able just to enjoy it. "The falling leaves, the smell of the forest..."

"It's beautiful," Toren said, gazing around as if he'd never seen anything like it.

"The best part is that all the mosquitoes are dead," Carina said cheerfully. "A few weeks ago, they would have driven us into the van in about ten minutes." She had to try very hard not to think about him shut in her van with her, or what they might do on the fold-down bed.

Shadow came with her on the second trip to the stream with a collapsible bucket for rinse water, and put his front feet in.

"If you go swimming, you are not stepping one foot into the van tonight," Carina warned him.

For a moment, she actually thought he understood her and was going to stay dry. Then he plunged into the stream, frolicking out into the flowing water and splashing her. "Argh!! That's *cold*!"

CHAPTER 4

Toren wished he'd accepted a drink. Something to do with his hands. Somewhere to look that wasn't *her*.

He nearly upended trying to get out of his camp chair again at Carina's cry of outrage, and he was standing before he realized that the stray dog had simply splashed her. It was easier to continue standing than to try to get back into the chair, so he came to help her up the bank from the stream.

"Can I...?"

"I've got it," she said firmly, but his hands were already outstretched to help her up the bank, and after the slightest hesitation, she put her free hand in his and let him haul her up, directly into his arms.

He hadn't meant to, but there she was, so close to him, and Toren wanted so badly to kiss her that he felt like his mouth was burning.

She was gazing up at him, her lips just parted, her hand still holding tight to his, her body against his, and Toren might have risked dipping his head to kiss her...if Shadow had not chosen that moment to come galloping up the bank to wedge his wet body between them.

They broke apart with exclamations of disgust, laughing as Shadow shook and sprayed them with cold creek water.

The moment of opportunity was gone and Toren desperately wanted that moment back. If he were suave like Fask, or smart like Rian, or funny like Tray, maybe he'd know what to do, how to get from this awkward place where they were to that place where he could tell her who he was...what *she* was.

Laughter died on his mouth.

She was his mate.

She was his *mate*.

And if he'd found his mate, he was first in line to be king. And not just the first *in line*, but they'd be jamming a crown on his head before *spring*.

Carina was kneeling by the fire, stirring the hot water in the cook pot with a few drops of camp soap and efficiently swiping out their bowls before rinsing them in the clear creek water.

"Want to help me dry?" she asked, and Toren startled from his thoughts. He wished he'd kissed her when he had the chance, because now he was alternating between cold terror and hot need in a wild seesaw, and there were emotions in his head that weren't his and he couldn't make sense of them.

"No!" he said, more firmly than he meant to. "I have to go."

Carina stood up, a towel in one hand and a chipped bowl in the other. "So soon?" she said, and Toren thought she was trying to say it humorously, but his ears were roaring.

"I'm sorry," he said, and he was, for the mess he was about to pull her into.

"Do I have to leave tonight?" Carina asked.

For a moment, Toren was confused, thinking she meant 'go back to the castle with him,' then he remembered that she thought he was just a ranger, evicting her from an illegal camping site.

"No," he said blindly. "No, stay here tonight. If anyone gives you trouble...tell them Toren said you could stay. But no one will. Give you trouble, I mean."

"Right," Carina said. Did she sound a little forlorn? Toren was having difficulty separating his own emotions from hers. "Thanks."

"Thanks for dinner," Toren said, reluctant to go, but at the same time desperate to escape.

Carina waved her towel at him. "My pleasure," she said flippantly.

Shadow looked from her to him, and back again, clearly picking up on the unexpected tension between them, and Toren bolted down the old road that Carina had driven the van up.

Toren had to walk quite a distance to find a space big enough to shift and take off in—landing was a little more contained, but lift-off required wingspan. It gave him far too much time to think about everything that was wrong with the whole situation...and everything that was right about Carina's smile, and her lithe body, and her sweet, brave laugh.

Then he was in the air, circling once above her and straining against his dragon's desire to return.

If she looked up, she would only see a shimmer in the air, a hint of the aurora against the deepening night sky.

He wanted nothing more than to dive into the clearing and scoop Carina up into his arms and tell her...what? That he was a dragon shifter? Oh, and not just any dragon shifter, supposing *that* revelation didn't send her running, but the youngest prince of Alaska? And then he'd have to explain that by meeting her, he'd just been selected to be king?

Would she want to be a queen? Toren wondered. Wasn't that the fantasy? Rags to riches? Van to castle?

But he pictured her, squatting next to the fire to stir noodles, remembered her simple, addictive delight in camp food and falling leaves. None of the riches he could offer her would ever cause so much uncomplicated joy.

And joy was all he wanted to give her.

He made himself fly back to the capital, over the wild forests and alpine swamps to Fairbanks, where the castle loomed in the hills west of the little city.

He didn't go straight to his own rooms, but landed on Rian's balcony, wings outspread to brake his flight. He shifted and knocked, then barged in, because the only thing Rian would have going on was a hot date with a book.

Rian looked up crossly from his computer. "Did you get rid of him?"

Toren stared blankly, then remembered his original duty. "No. I mean, it wasn't...Rian, I need your help."

CHAPTER 5

"Sure," Carina said, pouring a fresh bucket of water over the smoldering ashes. "Toren, the 'brand new park ranger,' gave me *personal* permission to camp on royal land. That excuse will go over great."

She didn't know who Toren really was, beyond *gorgeous* and *funny* and perpetually looking a little stunned, but she knew what he wasn't: a ranger. His arrival was weird, his departure even weirder, and Carina had been burned by *weird* too recently to feel good about it.

She wasn't going to wait around for whoever was going to come hassle her next. She'd felt inexplicably safe in his presence, but now that he was gone, all of the gravity of her situation had come tumbling back. And feeling *his* feelings? That was the most ridiculous part of it all.

"I should have stuck to the campgrounds," she told Shadow fiercely as she untied the tarp and dragged it to the widest space that she could find in order to fold it. "I should have stayed strictly legit." Shadow tried to walk out on it as Carina dragged one edge of the tarp to the other. "Get off, mutt!"

Shadow scampered away, his nails making the plastic rustle like the leaves that were swirling down to cover it as she folded the tarp.

"I should never have gotten complacent." The wood tools were thrown into the back of the van with the folded tarp and the messily coiled ropes.

"Idiot," she scolded herself as she folded her laundry and wound up the line. "You let yourself get lazy."

Alaska had been so beautiful and peaceful, so far away from people and bustling cities. It was easy to think that she could stay hidden for a while.

Shadow followed her from task to task, clearly puzzled by her strange human behavior. He sniffed the cold fire, and finally lay in front of the side door to the van. His message was clear: if Carina was leaving, he was, too.

Carina stepped over him to secure the built-in camp stove and switch the propane refrigerator to travel mode. Then she stretched up on her toes and pulled the bar that lowered the tented pop-top. In moments, the van was dark and snug, the canvas top tucked in and buckled into place.

For a moment, Carina sat on the back bench and looked around out of the windows, trying to recapture some of the peace and safety she'd felt when Toren was there.

Shadow cautiously crept up into the vehicle and put his head on her knee. She petted him before she realized that he was still wet from splashing in the creek. "Ugh. Alright, let's pull up our tent stakes and get out of here."

She pulled the door shut and Shadow whined from inside as she circled the van, turning off the propane and giving the dark campsite one last sweep with a flashlight; the shadows leaping away from her beam made Carina feel jumpy and nervous. Convinced that she wasn't leaving anything behind, she hopped into the driver's seat and started the van.

Shadow hopped into the passenger seat and sat, eagerly looking out of the windows.

"You are definitely not just a stray," Carina said, reaching over to scratch his ears as she adjusted the seat and turned on the headlights. It was very comfortable to have a travel companion.

She let herself indulge in a moment of imagination, picturing Toren in the seat beside her, remembering that queer feeling of safety and wholeness. She took her hand back from Shadow and put it firmly on the steering wheel.

Then she pointed the headlights back down the road she'd driven in on and set off. Again.

CHAPTER 6

"Promise you won't tell anyone," Toren begged. "Promise!"

Rian frowned at him. "Tor, you're being really weird."

That wasn't a promise; Rian had been extremely careful about making promises he didn't want to keep since the time his twin brother Tray had gotten him to agree to wear nothing but wool socks for an entire week. The rest of the palace had been scandalized by his nudity, and photographs of the prank had made it into an international gossip magazine and from there had spread to the Internet. Rian had very soberly declared that it served him right for being imprecise about the terms of the bet, and vowed never to let it happen again, but he wouldn't put clothing on until the week was up.

Because he had promised.

It was one reason Toren had come to him; if Rian promised to keep it quiet, he would.

"I'm not going to tell you until you swear not to tell anyone," Toren said fiercely.

Rian frowned. "If you're in trouble..."

"I am in so much trouble," Toren confessed, then he pressed his lips together firmly.

"What if it's something I feel obligated to report?" Rian asked.

Toren raised an eyebrow and narrowed his mouth further.

"What if I think that keeping it secret will make it worse?" Rian prodded.

Toren couldn't make his lips any thinner, but he tried.

"Fine," Rian conceded.

"Say it," Toren insisted, unwilling to get caught in any loopholes.

"I promise not to tell anyone unless..."

"Just promise not to tell!" Toren begged.

"I promise not to tell," Rian agreed reluctantly.

"Well, you know how father has been...indisposed for some time?"

It was an understatement. It wasn't unusual for older dragons to hibernate for periods of time, even as long as a year. But what had started as a lengthy nap had stretched into an unusual slumber, and then into a worrisome coma. They'd been trying to rouse him for several years now, without so much as a flicker of an eyelid.

"It has come to my attention," Rian said sarcastically.

To be fair, it hadn't been a problem at first; the king's position was largely for show and Fask had been able to step into his shoes with the barest public deflections about his father's health and travel.

"And you know how we need to have a king to send to the Compact Renewal before next summer?"

"Still with you, little brother."

"And you know how the next king is picked..."

Rian was starting to look more suspicious and less irritated. "If you listen to Fask, it's an outdated tradition.

Supposedly, the Compact shows the next king his mate and there's some ridiculously vague double-speak about sparking recognition. The Compact is tricky, though; I've never been sure it wasn't just a roundabout way of saying the king must be married."

"It's not," Toren said with absolute certainty.

Rian's stunned silence was a weak salve for the ratcheting discomfort that Toren was feeling. "You *met* your mate?"

"Her name is Carina, and she was the squatter I was sent to evict, and I've never felt like this before, and she thinks I'm a *park ranger* and Rian, I don't want to be the king and I don't know if she wants to be a queen or not, but I don't even know how to tell her I'm a dragon and she's *American* and I think I'm going to be sick."

"Well," said Rian practically, "if you're going to hurl, do it outside and don't get it on the books. Some of these are first editions."

Toren sat heavily down in a chair, not noticing the books on the cushion until his weight was on them. "Ouch."

Rian made a noise of protest as Toren upended the books onto the floor and flopped back into the chair.

"Where is she now?" Rian asked, looking around as if Toren had somehow smuggled her into the room without his notice.

"I left her at her camping spot…she's got one of those antique VW pop-up vans with the tent tops. It's a really nice set up, actually."

"Is she here on a visa? How long has she been here? Do you know anything about her family?"

Toren could only shrug.

"What does she know about you?" Rian scowled.

"She knows I'm an idiot who can barely sit upright in a camp chair," Toren groaned, running fingers through his short hair.

"She's really your mate?"

Toren's dragon gave a sigh of longing. "Oh, yeah," Toren agreed dreamily. "I looked into her eyes and it was...this...thing. I could see right into her soul. It was like this beautiful, crazy...thing." Orator, he was not.

"So, are you going to bring her here?"

That would be the logical thing, Toren knew. It was also pretty much the last thing he wanted to do. He wanted to hoard her to himself, to steal her and run away from all the complications finding her had added to his life.

Rian frowned, perhaps guessing his train of thought. "Okay, then...have you considered asking her on a date and asking her the kinds of questions you would ask a date?"

"A date?"

Rian gave a long-suffering sigh. "I don't know why you came to me for romantic advice," he said, shaking his head. "Wouldn't Tray have been better at this? Or *anyone*? But sure, a date. Take her to that Thai place downtown."

That was as good a plan as any. But, "What am I supposed to do about the...*king*...thing."

Rian frowned at that. "Well, I guess you'll be king."

Toren moaned. "No one wants that. Least of all me. Fask is the oldest, and he's the best at this."

Rian's frown softened. "It's not like we'd all leave you to do it alone, or anything. I mean, I guess it would pretty much just be a formality, no one would expect you to write contracts or anything."

"But only the king can attend the Compact Renewal. And I'd be expected to...do all those diplomatic dragon things..." Toren had only the vaguest idea what those things were; he'd always been happy that Fask enjoyed that kind of thing and that, as the youngest, Toren was generally expected to stay out of the way.

But even *he* knew that if the Compact wasn't renewed by

an Alaskan king, they'd be a target for take-over by the other kingdoms; their father's absence was becoming problematic, and many of their enemies were getting restless.

The Compact was the official document that laid out the alliance of the Small Kingdoms and protected the human countries...and the public copy of that document was a heavy tome of thick legal restrictions and trade agreements.

The *private* version of the Compact was a closely-guarded secret, shared only with the member royalty, and it was even longer, more involved, and steeped in structured magic. It was incredibly specific about successions and the power structure of the affiliated kingdoms. And one of the things that was laid out explicitly was that every king had a *mate*, chosen and confirmed by the Compact itself.

The document was periodically renewed, but never altered, and it enforced itself, *absolutely*. If Alaska couldn't send a king to the Renewal, they would be dropped from the alliance and lose the protections it offered.

"We'll teach you what to say and write your speeches," Rian assured him.

Toren tried to find the words for what was warring in his chest. He'd never loved the spotlight, but even more than that, he didn't want to let his brothers down. He didn't want to let the whole *country* down. They deserved a real king. The kind of king that could actually...rule. The kind of king their father had been.

If he had to wear a crown, he wanted to *earn* it, not just luck into it by finding his mate.

And his mate...

Toren couldn't stop *thinking* about Carina. He kept remembering the graceful way she moved, how brisk and efficient she was, how capable and funny and kind. She took in stray dogs and stray park rangers with equal aplomb, and served boxed macaroni and cheese like it had been specially catered for them.

He wanted desperately to do a date like Rian suggested... but just a date. No photographers, no uniforms, no crowns, no pressure. He wanted to find out what music she liked, where she'd grown up, and what she did for fun. Did she like hockey? Why was she so afraid? How could he protect her? He wanted to see if she tasted the way he imagined, hear what kind of noise she would make when he found all the places that made her blood run hot. He wanted to know if her lips were as soft as they looked, and whether she would...

Rian cleared his throat noisily and Toren realized that he'd been speaking for some time and Toren hadn't heard a word.

"Daydreaming?"

"I think you've got the right idea," Toren said apologetically. "I'll go ask her on a date. We can tell the others later, after I've had a chance to get to know her a little." He started to the balcony, but Rian stopped him.

"It's the middle of the night," he reminded Toren. "Maybe you should ask her in the morning, rather than barging into her campsite while she's sleeping."

Toren nodded and turned around, already trying to formulate his request. *Want to get a cup of coffee?* No, he wanted something better than that. *Will you accompany me to Fairbanks for dinner?* Way too formal.

Toren tripped over the books he'd left on the floor and sidetracked to put them back on the chair. "Thanks, Rian," he said absently, going to the door into the castle.

"Tor," Rian said warningly.

Toren paused in the doorway.

"Secrets are trouble," Rian said. "Secrets will only give you problems."

For a moment, Toren thought he meant keeping the

secret of his mate from his brothers, but Rian continued. "Tell her who you are. Especially who you are *now*. All of it."

Toren nodded slowly. "I will," he promised. "I will."

And then Rian did the most unnerving thing of all and bowed his head in unexpected respect.

Toren fled in terror.

CHAPTER 7

Carina pulled into Angel Hot Springs Resort at dawn and parked at the far end of the parking lot. "I'm going to have to get you a collar and a leash at some point," she told Shadow, who eagerly bounded out of the van to sniff for other dogs and stretch his legs.

Her van smelled like damp dog and Carina was surprised to find that she didn't really mind. She yawned. She'd taken a brief nap in a roadside pullout, but was still tired.

"I'm going to have to leave you in here for a little while," she apologized, when she shut Shadow back into the vehicle, and she spent a little time finger-combing the thick hair around his neck first. "You're such a good dog."

Shadow snuffled at her happily, his tail thumping against the back of the passenger seat. He seemed entirely content to stay behind in the van.

Carina took a duffel bag from the back of the van, stuffed a change of clothing, a bathing suit and toiletries into it, and slung it over her shoulder. She made sure the windows were all cracked for Shadow, who was already steaming them up with his hot breath in the crisp morning air.

She stood at the door to the pool house, frowning at her wavery reflection in the glass door. It was an hour until they opened, though she could see people moving around inside as they set up for the day.

"You left your camping spot."

Carina gave a startled yelp and swung around with her duffel bag slipping off her shoulder. She tried to catch it, and between her flailing snatch and the momentum of her turn, managed to slam it into Toren, who was suddenly, alarmingly, standing behind her.

He barely moved at the impact.

"Where did you come from?!" Carina demanded, her heart hammering in her chest. She tried to convince herself that it was only alarm, not the fact that he was even more handsome than she remembered, and standing distractingly close.

"I went back to find you this morning and you weren't there," Toren said, as if that explained anything.

"I was trespassing on royal grounds, remember? I didn't want to get in trouble. Did you *follow* me?" Carina couldn't make sense out of how he would have been able to track her.

"No," Toren said swiftly. "I waited until morning. I didn't want to wake you up, or scare you...though I have apparently done a poor job of not scaring you. And then...I just found you."

Carina wondered if he'd frightened her into shock. Her brain could not figure out how he had checked on her campsite that morning...and still managed to drive this far to find her. The sun was just barely rising over the hills around them now, so how did those logistics even work? Her brain really couldn't think of anything beyond the great, beautiful presence of him, and the way he filled up the shoulders of his uniform. His eyes didn't look any more blue in the early morning light than they had the night before; they were a shimmering silver-gray with crazy amounts of gemstone depth.

"Oh," Carina managed, when she realized that she'd been gazing into them for entirely too long. She grasped desperately for a topic of conversation. "Well, we're here too early. The pools don't open for another hour."

Toren scowled in through the glass doors. "They know me. They'll let us in," he said confidently, and sure enough, when he waved at the little gray-haired man who was busy behind the desk, he came to the door as soon as he saw Toren and unlocked it, starting to bob his head politely.

"You're..."

"We're early," blurted Toren firmly, cutting him off rather rudely. "But I was hoping that we could get in for a soak before breakfast. If it's not any *trouble*."

The man looked a little as if Toren had asked him to hold a snake. "I...er..."

"Not if it will get you into trouble," Carina said with a winning smile. "We can come back later."

The man looked at her, eyes wide, then back at Toren, then back at her, a slow, cautious smile pulling up his mouth that turned knowing. "No, my...er...ma'am. It's no trouble at all. Let me fetch you towels." He bowed them into the pool lobby so respectfully that for a moment, Carina wondered if he was mocking them.

"Being a park ranger has privileges," Carina remarked to Toren in a stage whisper.

She was looking at him, because she couldn't help it, and she caught a blush that betrayed him and made him look even cuter and more confused than ever, and she felt a wave of guilt from him.

"I'm...er...not..."

The man brought them three giant fluffy towels each, and showed them where the dressing rooms were. "Don't I need to buy a swim pass?" Carina asked quietly, eyeing the price chart above the desk. Towels were listed at five Alaskan dollars apiece, and access to the pools started at fifteen.

"I have a pass," Toren assured her, after he had exchanged a significant look with the towel-bearing man.

Carina wasn't going to look a gift towel in the mouth, and every dollar mattered, so she shrugged. "I'll...see you out at the pools, then."

The dressing room was absolutely magnificent, tiled in what looked like marble and jade, and trimmed in gleaming chrome. Framed mirrors were hung over a short row of sinks, and even the toilets looked like they were marble.

There weren't very many lockers, compared to the number of people that Carina's guidebook had led her to believe visited the springs, and each one was practically an individual closet. She picked one at random and stashed her belongings, hanging her towels on the hooks.

She shimmied into the bathing suit. It was her sister June's, and it was a practical plain-colored one-piece that she suddenly wished was something sexier. She wished *she* were a little sexier. Less skinny. Bigger breasts. Hair that didn't look like birds were nesting in it. She wished a lot of things were different about her life until she firmly lifted her chin and reminded herself that now was *now* and she was going to enjoy it, because things could definitely get worse.

Toren was already out in the room with the pools by the time she found the second entrance to the dressing room.

He hadn't gotten into one of the tubs yet, and Carina had to suck in her breath at the sight of him.

He was tall, and stood with an easy confidence that she had suspected was due to the park ranger uniform but clearly was *not*. His short, dark hair was standing up in spikes that indicated he had obeyed the signs mandating a shower before soaking. He had magnificently muscled arms, and shoulders, and legs, and...

Carina wasn't sure where he'd gotten his blue and gold shorts, as he hadn't been carrying a bag, but they left nothing to the imagination.

And he was looking at her like she was something edible, something that he was starving for, his silvery eyes shining in the low resort lighting. It even seemed like she could *feel* his desire.

He cleared his throat uncomfortably and Carina had to try very hard not to notice that his patriotic shorts were betraying his unmistakable interest. He moved the towel he was holding as subtly as he could manage to preserve his dignity.

"So, which pools do you recommend?" she asked, gazing around at the options. There were a number of small pools like hot tubs with various temperatures marked on electronic read-outs, and a large pool that might even be suitable for swimming, if it wasn't too warm. The whole room was steamy and finished to look like natural rock and landscaping, with tropical potted plants everywhere.

"None of these," Toren said swiftly. "Come see the outdoor pools."

The door to the outdoors was heavy and wooden, with a caribou antler handle. Toren opened it for Carina and stood aside while she stepped out into the bracing cold. "Oh, brrr!" Signs to a rock pool led her down a covered walkway, stepping lightly and quickly over the damp, steaming mats.

The walkway turned a corner and led down into a pool with a long, low ramp. The first step in was shocking, then it was utterly delicious and Carina waded eagerly out into it until she could duck down and put her whole body in, Toren splashing at her heels.

She had to wonder if the chilly walk had tamed his rising desire, but she didn't turn around soon enough to check.

It was just over waist-deep on her, sandy-bottomed, and pleasantly hot. It would be perfect to stand up and cool off just a little, and it was simple to crouch, or use one of the tiered underwater benches to sit with just her shoulders out of the water.

"This is amazing," Carina crowed, letting herself lean back into the water.

It had a slight mineral smell, but it wasn't as overwhelmingly sulfur-smelling as other hot springs she had visited. The pool was landscaped much as the interior pools had been, with rocks that looked mostly natural but were just a little too perfect. Instead of potted plants, there were small spruce trees planted all around so that the pool was shrouded and private from anyone who might be coming from any direction but inside the resort. It was just a little below freezing and the trees were sprinkled with shimmering ice crystals.

Fog wafted from the water, swirling thickly enough to obscure the far end of the pool, where Carina could hear running water.

"Carina..."

Toren wasn't appreciating the talent of the resort's landscaper or the beauty of the frosted trees.

He had followed her into the pool and was gazing at *her*, strange silver eyes gleaming. She couldn't tell what was his desire, or what was hers.

Impulsively, Carina floated towards him, and he put out his arms to catch her.

It was the most natural thing in the world to tip her head up for his kiss.

CHAPTER 8

She was the most beautiful woman that Toren had ever seen, her body absolutely intoxicating even in the practical, sport-style swimsuit she was wearing. The planes of her face, the modest swell of her breasts, the subtle curve of her hips…Toren had never seen anything he wanted more.

He remembered Rian's words. He didn't *want* to keep secrets from her. He wanted to tell her everything he was, give her everything he had, follow her anywhere, be anything.

"Carina," he started, ready to explain everything.

And then she swam into his arms and lifted her face to his, and he could do nothing but lean down to kiss her the way he'd been dying to since he first saw her brandishing a camp chair at him.

She was every single thing that he'd imagined the entire sleepless night before, her lips like electricity on his, her arms soft and strong and perfect. He could not stop kissing her to breathe, so desperate for her mouth, for the strangely intoxicating feel of her teeth against his tongue.

He could not get enough of how her arms around him felt, her fingers clawing at his shoulders as she drew him closer and wrapped a leg around him, pressing against the erection that he hadn't been able to hide or control.

He nearly drowned them both, trying desperately to hold her closer, to feel more of her, and kiss her more deeply, and they finally dragged apart from each other, panting and hot-eyed.

"Hot," said Carina, dazedly, and Toren realized that their frantic love-making had taken them into the hotter area of the pool. "So! Hot!"

"Mix the water," he advised. "The hot water sits on top, mix up from the bottom and it will be less painful." He glanced around, half-expecting to see a familiar figure materialize from the steam, but they were still alone in the pool.

She followed his advice, and the relief in her eyes was immediate. "Good trick," she said breathlessly.

There was a waterfall at this end of the pool, and they drifted towards it, kissing, floating, nearly falling over. They passed a set of stairs that were chained off, with a sign: "Upper pools reserved for the royal family of Alaska."

Carina gave the sign a curious look, and Toren wondered if this was his opportunity to bring up who he really was.

But Carina was dragging him past it to the waterfall before he could figure out how to explain; it wasn't like he could invite her to the upper pools anyway. It wasn't just a reserved luxury for royalty, those pools were usually many degrees hotter than human flesh could tolerate, and not even the royal family went there without an *invitation.*

Carina ducked into the waterfall, gasping at the cool, driving rush. "Oh," she said in pleasure, closing her eyes and letting it pound down over her head and shoulders. "It's as good as a massage," she said as she stepped away from it shaking her wet head.

Toren, unable to resist, gathered her into his arms and dragged her back into it, and they kissed deeply, the cooler water cloaking them.

When they broke apart at last, they ducked back into the water to warm up again, drifting back to the hotter areas. "You should come here when the weather is colder," Toren told her.

"Colder than this?" Carina protested. "I almost had a heart attack getting out here."

"It's brisker at thirty below," Toren teased. "But the pools feel even better. Everyone freezes their hair and beards into frosty shapes."

"Don't you get frostbite?" Carina said in wonder.

"The water keeps your core so hot, you can't get frostbite. And if your nose or ears feel cold, you can just duck them into the water."

"It's *magical*," Carina said, but she wasn't looking at the pools.

Toren pulled her back into his arms, turning her backwards so that he could simply hold her against him, burying his face into the side of her neck and wrapping her up tightly against him, as much of her against him as they could manage as they half-floated in the steam. It was like licking an ice cube in the face of terrible thirst—a tease of possible satisfaction, but so little compared to what he really wanted.

Patience, he told his dragon, and he had to laugh at the turn of events that had *him* cautioning patience. *She is ours.*

She is ours, his dragon agreed avidly.

"Toren," she said, twisting in his arms as she put her feet on the sandy bottom of the pool and stood. "Headrush…"

Then her eyes rolled back into her head, and Toren was catching her limp form.

They were back in the hottest part of the pool, Toren realized, and they'd been in the pools for most of the hour, making out avidly. He wasn't bothered by the heat, but she was only human, wasn't used to it, and on an empty stomach, probably dehydrated...

Toren gathered her into his arms and swept her up out of the pool.

CHAPTER 9

Carina came to as Toren waded up the ramp and the cold morning air touched her wet skin. She'd been so hot…and now she was so cold. She shivered and wrapped her arms around Toren. He was bare out of the pool in a way that he hadn't seemed to be when they were submerged together, and his skin was warm and safe.

The resort had opened to the public for the day, and there were tourists and local users starting to come in; they stared at Carina, being carried out of the pool by this tall, gorgeous guy like she was a feather.

"You can put me down," she said, embarrassed. The dizziness had passed.

Toren refused to do so, until they'd gotten through the antler-handled door into the pool room, where he laid her down on a padded lounge chair. "I'm such an idiot," Carina murmured.

"Someone get her a bottle of water," Toren commanded, not taking his eyes off of her, and several people scattered away.

"I'm fine," Carina insisted, but when she tried to sit up, Toren put a gentle, immovable hand on her shoulder.

"Rest," he said. "I shouldn't have let you stay out there so long."

"You're not the boss of me," Carina reminded him. Then, more quietly, she added, "Anyway, we were having fun…"

Toren's face split into a boyish grin. "Yeah," he said, his face coloring.

Someone brought a towel, which Toren insisted on putting under her head, and he let her sit up to gulp down most of a bottle of lukewarm water.

"Better?" he asked.

"Yeah," Carina said. "I was stupid. They have signs all over the place about drinking water and not staying in too long."

"It happens," Toren said comfortably, twining his fingers in hers possessively.

The little crowd that had gathered slowly dispersed as it became clear that Carina was not (to their disappointment, she was sure) going to die dramatically. They wandered away to their own soaking, whispering and speculating.

"We should get some breakfast in you," Toren said decisively, and for one wicked moment, that was not at *all* what Carina wanted in her.

But eating some food was probably much smarter than dragging Toren back into the water for more hot not-a-ranger make-out time. "There's a really great restaurant at the resort," Toren told her.

"That sounds like a good idea," Carina agreed. "Right now, I'd eat my hiking boots and my dirty socks sound delicious."

They walked back to the dressing rooms they'd come in through together and Toren reluctantly let her go into the ladies room alone. "If you aren't out in ten minutes, I'm sending someone in to get you," he warned her.

"Make it fifteen," Carina said. "I want to wash my hair."

Toren frowned, but agreed, and to her surprise, bent to give her a quick, possessive promise of a kiss that somehow didn't strike Carina as presumptuous. "Fifteen," he agreed.

Not for a moment doubting that Toren would indeed send someone in after her, Carina rushed through untangling her braid, washing, and conditioning it. To her surprise, the shower stalls were stocked with product that was far higher quality than what she'd brought...and no one else was in the dressing room whatsoever. There weren't even any swim bags lying about, or any towels but her own, untouched.

She showered swiftly, found some spray in conditioner for her hair, brushed it fiercely, and blew it halfway dry before she realized she hadn't looked at the time when she came in. She dressed in her last clean change of clothes, left the towels in an empty wicker hamper, and was out in the lobby...by herself. A few tourists were looking over the postcard display on the counter, but Toren was nowhere in sight.

The tourists were directed to completely different dressing rooms than Carina had just come out of, their swim passes firmly in hand and towels of a much lesser grade than she and Toren had gotten over their arms.

Toren must have a helluva pool pass, Carina thought suspiciously. She came to look over the postcards on the counter. Maybe she'd send one to her sister, she thought. Then she remembered that she couldn't and put the one she'd picked up back in the rack, tamping down her worry with resolve.

Then she caught sight of the postcard behind it and she felt a rush of dizziness not unlike the one that had sent her swooning into Toren's arms.

It was a portrait postcard, with a caption that said, "The royal family frequently enjoys visiting Angel Springs Resort." It was dated four years ago.

It featured a silver-haired, bearded man who was clearly the king, looking absolutely, undeniably kingly in a *very* familiar uniform indeed, standing near the rock entrance to the resort. Ranged beside him were six young men that Carina recognized from the brochure in her van. The oldest two still looked like they didn't care to be standing next to one another, one of the twins still looked bookish and the other looked like a jock, the only blond of the bunch looked like he was in a staring contest with the camera...and the youngest one was very definitely not a child any more.

Toren's silver eyes and grin were unmistakable. He was not the shortest one any longer, though he wasn't the tallest, but he was by far the most irreverent-looking.

He was also, Carina thought furiously, the best-looking of them, and her kiss-swollen lips burned.

CHAPTER 10

"I have to go," Toren said shortly into the phone, glancing at his watch. He wasn't sure if fifteen minutes had actually passed or not, since he'd failed to take note of the time he'd left Carina at the dressing room door, but he knew that every moment he spent away from her company left him feeling bereft.

"Fask wants to know if you got rid of the squatter," Tray said from the phone. "Just give me something to tell him, baby brother."

"The squatter has moved on," Toren said, ignoring the subtle slight. "No problem." It was the literal truth.

"So you'll have time to help me coordinate the visit of the King and Queen of Mo'orea," Tray said brightly. "Great! I think that Fask is interested in their daughter—"

"No!" Toren said in alarm. Sitting down with the press secretary to plan a formal dinner and entertainment did not fit in with his plans to find somewhere nice and lay Carina down in a pile of rose petals.

"Look, I know you want to go hunting, or playing hockey,

or whatever it is you do when you're shirking your family duties, but Fask isn't wrong about us doing..."

"Later," Toren promised vaguely. For a moment anger and frustration slashed through him. He wished he could just be *normal*.

Bad enough that he came with a giant nosy family. Bad enough that he was going to have to explain to Carina that he was a dragon shifter. But on top of that, that he'd have to be *king*?

And that meant she *would* be queen.

It wasn't a suggestion, it was a mandate. They would bring her to the coronation in irons if that's what it took to save Alaska.

And Toren already guessed that Carina didn't particularly like to be told what to do.

Whatever Tray said, something about *duty* and *responsibility*, was swept away when he came out of the dressing room and found Carina standing in the lobby.

If she had been beautiful with her unkempt braid and soot-smudged cheeks, she was now a goddess. Long, loose blonde hair fell in damp waves nearly to her waist, and she was wearing a jumper over thick striped tights showing off her long, strong legs, an insulated plaid flannel shirt several sizes too big over that. She had the duffel bag she had tried to accost him with at the door over one shoulder and she was standing at the counter looking fixedly at something in her hands.

Her nose was straight in profile, her kiss-hungry mouth pulled into a tight, thoughtful pout.

Then she turned and saw him. Her hazel eyes flashed gorgeously and Toren recognized the heightened level of beauty in her face as fury even as he *felt* it.

"Gotta go," he said frantically, trying to thumb off his phone without looking at it.

She was holding a postcard, one that Toren had signed a hundred copies of at least, and he could not hope that she hadn't recognized him.

Not the way she was glaring at him now.

"Should I curtsy?" she asked in frigid tones.

"You don't have to curtsy," Toren said with a sigh.

"I suppose 'you were going to tell me,'" she scoffed.

Toren had been meaning to, but he suspected that saying as much wouldn't help him much now. He tried a charming smile. "Want to go have breakfast with me?"

"If I decline Your Majesty, will your guards have me arrested?"

Toren actually glanced around to see if his honor guards had shown up, then realized she was only joking. Angry-joking.

"You don't have to," he said. "I just want you to. I've got… wow, I've got a lot to tell you. Anyway, it's Your Highness, not Your Majesty." *For now.*

She seemed to be expecting more resistance, or maybe guilt, but Toren was only glad. This had saved him having to explain one thing, even if he had a bucket of other incredible explanations to try to make. Rian was right, he thought, keeping secrets was only trouble, and he was looking forward to coming clean about everything.

"Want me to sign your postcard?" he offered with a grin.

She stared at him in astonishment. "I'm still mad at you," she said, putting the postcard back. "And I have to let Shadow out."

"Can I come with you?"

She swept an exaggerated bow. "Yes, Your Majesty, please come to my humble van so that my noble hound can go *pee.*"

"Thank you, My Lady," Toren replied with perfect courtesy, giving her an equal bow with a hand flourish.

He dashed ahead of her to open the door, and she followed him bemusedly.

"I knew you weren't a ranger," she grumbled, but the corners of her mouth were twitching.

"I never said I was," Toren reminded her.

She came to a complete stop. "You don't think that's the same as honesty, do you?" she asked narrowly, every trace of her humor gone.

Toren soberly came to a stop with her. "It isn't," he said firmly. "And I should have figured out how to tell you sooner. I'm sorry."

She blinked at him. "You are full of surprises," she said, frowning.

"Some of them are good, I hope," Toren said, giving his most charming smile.

"I haven't decided yet," she said, but Toren caught the reluctant smile on her face before she stalked ahead of him to her van.

But when they got there, Shadow was gone.

CHAPTER 11

Carina wandered around the van, poking into the underbrush. "Shadow, here Shadow!" She had left one of the side windows open and the ajar screen suggested how he had escaped.

Toren, in very unprincely fashion, joined her, calling and whistling, and they walked the length of the parking lot.

"He's not even my dog," she reminded herself unhappily.

"I'll help look for him more after breakfast," Toren suggested. "And we'll report him missing at the front desk of the resort.

"Don't you have more important princely things to do?" Carina asked, and Toren winced and felt guilty, as if she had struck a nerve.

"They can wait," he said firmly. "None of them are more important than this."

"I *am* really hungry," Carina admitted. She also really didn't want to faint in front of Toren again. As unexpectedly lovely as it had been to gain consciousness in his careful embrace, she didn't care to repeat the spectacle.

"Your Highness," they were greeted at the door to the

restaurant, and Carina abruptly realized that man who had let them into the pools that morning had not been starting to say 'You're early...' or 'You're not allowed...' but 'Your.' As in Your *Highness*.

Feeling stupid made her scowl, and the server quickly added, "My Lady," and raked her with a gaze as if he was desperately trying to find some symbol of her rank on her insulated flannel.

"A private table," Toren said confidently.

"Yes, Your Highness."

They were led through a small, quaint restaurant to not only a private table, but an entire private room, with a large central table and a few smaller satellite tables. None of them were set, but there were rather suddenly three servers frantically putting out candles and cloth napkins at one of the small tables.

"We sometimes come here for holiday parties," Toren explained.

"Well sure," Carina said casually, keenly aware of her ten dollar dress and striped tights. "And when the president of the United States visits."

Toren was quiet so long that Carina realized that he probably *had* entertained the president in this room.

"Never mind," she choked. Their seats were ready and the servers stepped aside to let Toren slip her chair back and tuck her into place. He was then seated by one of them, and heavy cloth napkins were spread into their laps.

Everyone moved in easy, practiced patterns, and Carina felt like she was in one of the OCD memes on the Internet, the one tile that didn't match.

There was a full spread of cutlery, and wine glasses full of ice cubes and water and Carina wasn't sure what to use. Then, to her amazement, she was being handed a hot towel with a pair of tongs.

She mimicked Toren, who wiped his hands and put the towel back on the tray being held for him.

"I bet this isn't the service they get in the main room," she joked.

Then she was handed a menu that she was very certain they did not offer to anyone in the rest of the restaurant. The choices included king salmon and king crab and bacon-wrapped moose tenderloins and truffles and some things in French that Carina didn't even recognize. There were no prices listed.

If you have to ask...

She *did* have to ask. "You were going to *tell* me, right?"

Toren put down the menu he'd been studying and looked earnestly into her eyes. "I was going to tell you. I want to tell you everything."

The server's approach kept them from continuing that train of thought.

"Can I get you something to drink?" she asked courteously.

"Coffee," Carina said. "Nothing fancy. In fact, the worst coffee you have, please. Instant, if you've got it. I don't want to ruin my tastebuds for camp coffee."

Toren grinned at her. "Coffee," he agreed. "Something a step above that, please."

"Do you know what you'd like for breakfast?" the server asked, smothering a smile.

Carina glanced over the menu again. "Can I just get an ordinary omelet with lots of veggies and cheese and some toast?"

"Sourdough, white, wheat, or bagel?" the server prompted, her face serene again.

"Sourdough seems appropriate," Carina deadpanned in return.

Toren ordered crab eggs Benedict.

And then they were alone in the fanciest restaurant that Carina had ever seen from the inside. The servers had lit the candles, which seemed a little inappropriate for breakfast, but she had to admit that it was atmospheric. There were a few windows letting in midmorning light, filtered through lace curtains.

"So... why me?"

Toren's eyes really were silvery, barely blue at all. "Why what?"

"After you evicted me from royal grounds...why'd you follow me? And for that matter, *how*? I never saw a car, yesterday, and it took me hours to drive here. But mostly...why?"

He took a bracing breath. "Because you are my mate."

"Ow ya goin', mate?" Carina replied in a dead perfect Australian accent.

CHAPTER 12

Whatever Toren had grimly expected a mate to be, it was not whooping laughter over lace tablecloths, or Carina's straight-faced humor, or the way her eyes would crinkle at the corner whenever something amused her. He had never found a face like hers, so interesting and expressive that he simply wanted to watch it, and never let it out of his sight because it was possible he'd miss something there, and that thought broke his heart.

He wanted her, like he thought he would be attracted to a mate, but he never expected *wanting* to be like this, a strange mix of physical need and emotional longing and deep contentment in her presence. He was starting to realize that a lot of what he was feeling wasn't entirely his own, either; he could feel her reactions to things. Even weirder, there were moments when he felt like he'd known her for years, with all the attendant comfort of familiarity, not just a few awkward hours.

Almost like he was feeling what he *would* feel for her after they'd been together for a very long time.

"So, no," she insisted, once they had both gotten their laughter under control and she'd used a corner of her linen napkin to wipe her eyes. "Why'd you follow me?"

"I'm serious," Toren said, but then their breakfasts were served.

"That was fast," Carina said in surprise. "And that is not an ordinary omelet."

It was a beautiful omelet, fluffy and folded full of fresh chopped vegetables. When she cut into it, it oozed three colors of cheese, and there were perfect circles of green onion scattered over it. There was a side of berries—tiny wild strawberries and blueberries. Carina looked at them dubiously, undoubtedly comparing them to their much larger and grander—and far blander—commercial varieties, then tasted one.

Her eyes widened. "Good things come in little packages," she observed. She ate all of hers, and then all of his, when he offered them, then tucked away her omelet with earnest good will.

"You're my mate," Toren tried again, after a few false starts around his own fine food. "It's not Australian, and it's not crazy. Well, it's all going to sound a little crazy, so hear me out, okay?"

"I'm sitting here eating with royalty after kissing you in a hot springs pool and fainting in your arms," Carina reminded him. "Crazy appears to be the theme of the day. Hell, it's the theme of my life lately." She mopped up some stray cheese with her toast and Toren felt a wave of frustration and fear that wasn't his own.

"Well... you know how they call my dad the Dragon King of Alaska?" Toren attempted to act casual.

"Crazy," Carina muttered under her breath, but she gestured Toren to continue as she picked up her water glass.

"We're actually dragons."

Carina's eyes met his over the rim of her glass, and to her credit, she continued drinking without spilling it on herself. "You don't look like a dragon."

"We're dragon shifters, we can take either form at will. But there's something else..." Toren sucked in a breath.

"Something more than *being a dragon*."

"A king is chosen by...well, it's magic. Dragons chosen to lead don't do so alone; there is always a ruling *pair*. They have to find their true mate in order to be a true king; they won't be accepted by the Compact if they don't have their queen at their side."

"A true *mate?*" Toren could see her reconsidering her Australian joke.

"For me, that's you, and I recognized you as soon as I saw you, and I don't ever want to be without you again."

Though her hand was shaking just a little, Carina managed to get the glass down to the table. It thumped down harder than she probably intended.

"Like love at first sight?" she said thinly.

"Not always. It can be people who've known each other. No one exactly knows how or when or why a mate bond gets activated, just that it always happens when one of the kingdoms needs a ruler. It's all written out in the secret version of the Compact, something about *fertile ground* and *great need*."

"Anything else?" she asked dryly.

"Because I'm the only one of my brothers to *have* a mate, I am now the *crown* prince, and they'll need me to marry and be crowned king before summer so that I can sign the Compact Renewal and save our country..."

Her face lit up and her eyes narrowed into laughter for a moment until she realized that Toren wasn't laughing with her, and she immediately sobered. "You can't be serious. I mean...you warned me about crazy, but that takes the cake."

Toren was full of relief. Rian had absolutely been right:

secrets were nothing but trouble and he felt like there was a great weight off of his shoulders.

Even if she really didn't look like she actually believed him and he could feel her waves of doubt.

"I'm not really queen material," Carina said slowly.

"I beg to differ," Toren said. "But honestly, I'm not really king material. Any of my brothers would be better at it. I haven't told anyone but Rian yet and I'm absolutely dreading it."

"We just met," Carina protested. "This is..."

"I know," Toren said, knowing that he was smiling foolishly at her.

"What do you think happens now?" Carina asked with deep skepticism.

"Come to Fairbanks with me," Toren said thoughtfully. "Meet the family." That was the right thing to do, no matter how much he didn't want to do it. No secrets.

Carina put her forehead in her hand and gave a tired sigh. "Just *supposing* that this isn't some kind of heat-induced hallucination, did you consider that your family won't want me for a queen?"

At the last moment, Toren kept himself from blurting that they didn't have a choice. Maybe he *was* getting better at diplomacy. "They'll love you," he assured her. "Like I do."

Carina's eyes shot to his, wide and alarmed. "We *just* met," she repeated. "You don't even know me."

Toren reached across the table and took her un-resisting hands in his own. "Carina..."

"Even if I was willing to marry you after one hot make-out session in a pool, you should know..." She paused, her hazel gaze skidding away from his and Toren could sense her fear.

"It doesn't matter."

"It kind of does," Carina said, looking up through her eyelashes at him. "Since Alaska undoubtedly has an extradition agreement with the United States and I'm pretty sure I'm wanted for murder."

CHAPTER 13

Carina took a certain amount of pleasure in the disbelief in Toren's face. It was about time that she was able to dish a little of that back, after his outrageous revelations about being royalty and a dragon, by the way.

It was all completely implausible and Carina could feel her brain trying to accept the information, circling around the facts, and the evidence, and all the beautiful, crazy possibilities.

"You are not a murderer," Toren said with comforting conviction. His belief in her innocence unwound something tight in Carina's chest that she hadn't realized was there.

They both fell awkwardly silent as one of the servers came into the room to take their plates.

Once the server had refilled their waters and left them alone again, Carina looked speculatively at Toren and tried to figure out where to go from there.

She believed that he was the prince of Alaska; it was a little insane, but service like this, his face on a postcard, everything about his bearing...it was undeniable.

The revelation of dragon-people, that was a little more of a stretch.

And being his soulmate was a *ridiculous* idea.

Except...

Carina closed her eyes.

She had never reacted to anyone the way she responded to him. It wasn't just the way he set her body on fire. And it wasn't just the way he was so good looking it almost made her ache to look at him.

It was the way she felt safe with him, the way nothing had felt safe in such a long time. It was the way that she wanted to tell him everything, to unlock the secrets that were thick on her tongue.

It was like magic.

Because it *was* magic. That's *all* it was. It was actually comforting, having a reason for her crazy-intense emotions, for the way she could imagine she was feeling his emotions and staring into his very soul.

He was still holding onto her, making lazy circles on the backs of her hands with his thumbs.

"Hey, hey, you want to go for a walk and tell me about it?"

She desperately wanted to tell him everything. Did he have any idea what a turmoil she was inside? Did he guess how desperately she was clutching at humor to keep from breaking down? Was he feeling her emotions the way she seemed to feel his?

"Yeah," she said quietly. "Let's go for a walk."

They shed their heavy napkins. Toren made no motion to pay or leave a tip. Carina idly wondered if they paid a monthly fee, or if the royal family would be billed later. Maybe they actually owned the place. She swallowed back the hysterical laughter that bubbled up in her throat.

Carina went for the door they'd come in, but Toren

caught her hand. "Let's go out the back," he suggested. "Our pictures are probably already online."

"Our...pictures?" Carina had a stab of terror. She was supposed to be keeping a low profile until she could figure out her next steps, not letting photographs of herself out on the Internet where they might be seen by all the wrong people.

"I think some people noticed when I carried you out of the pool. I bet that the Prince Toren Fan Page is already wild with speculation."

Carina could not quite keep her unladylike snort to herself. "There's a Prince Toren Fan Page? On Facebook?"

Toren blushed. "Ah...yeah."

"Is it popular?"

He blushed further, confirming Carina's suspicion that it was.

"I'm tempted to join," she teased him. "And post about how hopeless you are at making campfires or sitting upright in a basic chair."

"Don't do it," Toren begged. "Some of the admins are really catty and I wouldn't be able to resist posting in your defense, and then they'd ban me, and that would be really embarrassing on my own fan page." His silver eyes were dancing.

Carina laughed. "I won't do it. I'm staying off of Facebook anyway. Wanted for murder, remember? I threw out my phone before I drove into Canada."

"You have a hell of a story to tell me," Toren said, frowning at her.

"It's not as good a story as being a dragon shifter and in line for the throne because of a magic spell," Carina told him, not sure if she was joking or not.

They passed one of the servers as they snuck out the back. "Thanks," Carina told her, waving. "It was delicious!"

The afternoon was glorious, a perfect Alaskan autumn day. A slight breeze rustled the leaves that remained on the trees, and the light over the hills around them was golden and warm.

And Toren's hand in hers, mate nonsense or not, was the most wonderful feeling Carina could remember.

They stopped briefly at the gift shop and Carina, in a moment of hopefulness, bought a souvenir leash and dog collar in dark blue with gold stars all over it. They stopped again at the van and called hopefully around for Shadow with no luck.

Twice, she tried to start telling her story to Toren, but they ran into people and were driven to silence.

"This way," Toren said, taking her by the hand.

There was a marked trail to the ridge of one of the nearby hills, which gave them a wide view of the valley through the trees as they climbed the boardwalk. They passed another couple, and the woman grasped her partner's hand and stared at Toren with recognition and unabashed curiosity.

It was quite unnerving.

And just a little bit fun.

Then Carina remembered that Toren thought she was going to be an honest-to-God *queen* and it seemed a lot less fun.

"This way," Toren said unexpectedly, as they walked through a stand of dark spruces. He tugged her off the trail behind a frame of rock outcroppings and a sign that explicitly warned hikers not to leave the trail and they scrambled together up a trackless slope and over a short ridge.

"Where are we going?" Carina asked breathlessly, letting him pull her up over a rock about the size of her van.

"There's a place I want to show you..." he said, leading her along a barely visible trail.

Then they burst out of a narrow crevice onto a meadow, dressed in russet seasonal colors.

"It's beautiful," Carina said, gazing over the rustling grasses. The far end was fringed in dark evergreens, and she could see the distant glimmer of a pond. There was something about the land that made her feel like she was exactly where she was meant to be.

"I found this place when I was trying to get away from my brothers," Toren told her. "We used to come here a lot...when my father was awake."

His father. His father the *king*.

Carina shivered and folded her arms around herself. She buttoned the collar button of the oversized flannel she was wearing, and sat down on a mossy boulder. "Well, you've told me your crazy story, let me tell you mine."

CHAPTER 14

Carina's unrest was like sitting on a porcupine, Toren thought. She felt like prickles of doubt and fear and despair. He wished he could protect her from all of it.

"I was an accountant, for a big company in Portland," Carina started, as she settled down onto a moss-cushioned rock. "I was fairly new, but there were some job promotions that were coming open and I really wanted a chance at them. So I was taking all the overtime projects, working late and trying to convince my bosses that I was lower middle management material by showing initiative."

Toren, suspecting a lengthy tale, took a seat next to Carina and put his arm around her. Her unrest felt prickly but after a moment, she leaned into him and all the sharp edges smoothed.

"I was working late one night. You know the drill: creepy music, empty hallways, the sound of that one janitor down the hall that you never see. And we have a client, a big client. It's a bank I guarantee you've heard of. We were doing some routine independent review of their financials, and we had access to necessary non-sensitive customer data. Like, we got the bank account numbers and the dates the account were created, and the financial transaction lists, but not their name or contact information."

"You found something," Toren guessed.

Carina gave a hiccup that he thought was meant to be a laugh but didn't quite make it.

"Mostly, we use this interface that crunches the data, but I like seeing things in charts, so I pulled up the raw database. And, I'm skimming through some accounts, looking for the ones that were flagged for review, and I noticed...a whole bunch of accounts were exactly the same. Not their balances, but their account creation dates. The interface just shows you a month and year of creation, so you'd never notice anything weird from there, plenty of accounts are created every month. But the database saves a time-date stamp, and these were all created within about twenty seconds of each other. Not just a few accounts, but spontaneously this bank had like three hundred new accounts and all of them had money in them. None of them individually had enough to raise any flags, none of them more than a hundred thousand. Some of them were even really small. But I added balances up and there was over five million US dollars sitting in these fabricated accounts."

"Money laundering?" Toren barely knew what money laundering was, but he knew enough to recognize that something was very wrong with what Carina was describing.

"Well, at first, I thought it might just be a spontaneous buyout...like maybe they'd acquired a smaller bank or something? So I started looking further. We had about eighteen months of data, from just one of their geographic locations, and I found three clusters of these accounts. And that made me think, how long had this been going on? I was looking at almost fifteen million in imaginary money in a relatively short window of time for just their Pacific coast branches. So

I called the bank and told them we were missing some of the data we needed for analysis and I asked..." Carina caught her breath and Toren could feel guilt threaten to swamp her. He tightened his embrace, and after a moment she could go on.

"I asked the secretary I got on the phone to send me the files going back further, and I took a chance and asked for the information from other districts, too. And she hemmed and hawed about policy and privacy and...I told her what I'd found, and what I was actually looking for. She was scared. She didn't want to get involved, and I didn't think she was going to, but a few days later, she called me back."

"She gave me her direct number, and sent me the files I needed on a flash drive by courier. She said that she'd started looking deeper from her end, and that she could confirm that there hadn't been any buyouts at the times these accounts were created.

"And I was right, there were more of these account clusters, going back years, all over the world. *Billions* of dollars. Sitting there, invisible, in these perfectly legit looking accounts that had been created by someone at the very top of the company. I was holding a bomb, and I knew it." Carina was shivering now.

Not sure what else to do, Toren took off his uniform coat and wrapped it around her, even though he knew it wasn't because of the cold.

She cuddled into the blue coat. "Well, *they* knew it now, too. When I got the flash drive, I called to thank her, and tell her what else I'd found, but she wasn't the one who answered. It was a man's voice, and he started asking questions. I hung up in a blind panic."

Carina's voice was growing raw. "I said I had a headache and went home early, but instead of going home, I went to my sister's place and told her everything. She gave me lunch and put me in a shower, and when I came out, there were men in suits at the door asking about me. I hid in the hall, listening, while they told her that the secretary at the bank had been found dead and they wanted me for questioning."

"I knew my sister was good on her feet, way better than me, but I didn't realize how good she was until I saw her deflect those guys. They wouldn't show badges, and didn't have a warrant, and my sister brushed them right off. The flash drive, with the Amco Bank logo, was sitting right out on the table behind her, too."

"Wait," Toren stopped her. "*Amco Bank?*"

"I told you you'd heard of them," Carina said wryly.

"That's one of the largest banks in the world," Toren said in horror, beginning to glimpse the scope of her problem.

"Exactly. June, that's my sister, she gave me her passport, because we look enough alike to pass, and her van, which she'd packed to go camping with her boyfriend that weekend, whatever cash she had, and I threw out my phone and drove north. I haven't...I haven't been able to contact her since then. I figured it was safer for her if I didn't."

"And you came to Alaska."

"I needed to stay low for a while, find someone who could help me out," Carina said. "I thought maybe I could find a journalist who would take the story and blow it wide open. And Alaska is where you go to get lost."

"You came here to be *found*," Toren said with utter conviction. "I'll make some calls when we get back to the resort, and we'll check on your sister. We'll see if there even *is* a warrant out for you, and Rian will know how to get you diplomatic immunity if there is. We've got an international lawyer who can represent you, if it comes to a trial."

She looked into his face, and Toren didn't even need to feel the emotions to see the tangled up fear and relief in her eyes. "I feel so stupid for getting mixed up in this."

"It wasn't stupid," Toren told her. "It was brilliant. You're smart and you're ethical. We'll make everything right. You don't have to be strong by yourself anymore."

Carina turned to bury her face in his shoulder, shaking. "I feel like this is all so surreal. Like I'm stuck in a dream that can't decide if it's a horror or a fantasy. Wanted for murder, magically in love with a prince...make up your mind!"

"I can only promise it has a happy ending," Toren said, pushing her hair behind her ear and kissing her temple. He desperately wanted to do more than just kiss, but then he thought of something that might cheer her up even more.

"Do you want to go for a quick flight?"

CHAPTER 15

Carina was puzzled at the offer, then abruptly remembered that Toren was a *dragon*. It still seemed utterly unreal. But the weirdest part was that she could *feel* his confidence in the idea. He didn't think he was lying. He wasn't deceiving her. She wasn't sure he *could* deceive her.

And she didn't think she could deceive him, either.

"I'd...like that?" she agreed cautiously.

He stepped back carefully, gave a curious ripple and then suddenly expanded into space, spreading wings like giant sails into the air over Carina's head. He was bejeweled, with scales that shimmered with a thousand different dark rainbow hues at every subtle shiver of his hide, and his long, graceful neck was arched so that he could regard Carina from giant, dark eyes that seemed to glimmer with very distant coals. His nose was long, and when his mouth opened in a way that was somehow similar to Toren's human grin, there was a row of teeth, each one the size of Carina's hand.

His wings moved with flexible precision, and he sat up on hind legs the height of Carina herself to extend a... paw? claw? There were three digits facing forward and one opposable that suggested a thumb, and all of them were tipped in curved claws the size of Carina's head. She cautiously touched one; it looked like gemstone and was warm under her fingers.

Toren crouched then, turning his side to her and folding his wings back.

Carina hesitated.

His nearest wingtip swept out, gesturing toward his shoulder.

Carina buttoned the toggles on Toren's big uniform jacket, then stepped close. She put her hand up on his elbow, and scrambled ungracefully up to throw her leg over him and straddle the ridge of his back. The position keenly reminded her of their kissing adventure in the pool earlier, and the fact that they'd never done anything about the tension they'd ratcheted up.

Toren gave a little shake that reminded Carina exactly how far above the ground she was and she settled herself more firmly against him, leaning forwards. This close, she realized that the scales were actually very knobby and textured, and that there were very natural handholds all over his hide. She found two good grips, pressed close to Toren's neck.

Toren gave an experimental bounce that took Carina's breath away, then sprang into the air with a whoosh of broad, leathery wings.

She was glad she had been lying almost prone at take-off, because the press of the air as they rose up would have flattened her. At first, it was all she could do to catch her breath, to keep her balance, and not lose her grip on scales.

Then, slowly, she dared to open her eyes and lift first her head and then her torso.

The land below her was brilliant folds of yellow-gold birch and dark evergreen, spun through with ribbons of rivers and set with precious gems of lakes and ponds. They were high enough now to see snow-capped mountains. Carina tried to remember what they must be from her vague understanding of Alaskan geography. The White Mountains?

The wind was making her eyes tear; she would have to get aviator's goggles if she was going to make a habit of this, she thought, giggling.

Toren tipped then, banking into a slow, gentle curve that felt anything but slow or gentle to Carina. She clung for dear life and pressed her head back down to Toren's neck. Her thighs ached from squeezing, and she was glad to recognize the meadow they'd taken off from through her streaming tears.

Toren landed so gently that it was almost anticlimactic, and Carina carefully released her cramping hands and half-fell down his side.

Riding a dragon wasn't exactly the Never Ending Story sequence with arm raised in victory, and Carina found that she'd broken two of her nails and scraped herself in several places. Her hair was sticking out in every direction, tangled impossibly, and her ears were bitterly cold.

Still, "That was amazing!" she crowed, swaying in place as her stressed thighs remembered how to hold her upright again. "*Amazing!*"

There was an odd, sudden suction of air, and then Toren was standing beside her, looking entirely self-satisfied.

"Won't people see you when you do that?" Carina asked, trying to tame her hair with her fingers.

"They'll only see a little shimmer in the sky if they look up during the *day*," Toren explained, closing the distance between them.

Cloaking magic. Sure, why not, Carina thought. There were dragons and mates, after all.

"What would they see at night?" she asked, suddenly hearing the specifics in Toren's explanation.

"Can't you guess?" he teased.

"Northern lights," Carina said, laughing. "Of course. I saw them the evening you came to evict me."

"There are real ones, too," Toren said modestly.

Carina wasn't making much progress with her hair. She managed to tangle her fingers into it and had to wiggle them out. "You know what people are going to assume if I come back looking like this, don't you," she scolded Toren.

"That you went riding on a dragon?" he teased.

"I think they'll guess something a little more mundane first," Carina told him shyly, toying with the toggles on his uniform coat.

Toren's grin went wider. "It would be a shame to raise those kinds of expectations with no basis in reality," he suggested, and to Carina's delight, he bent to kiss her.

CHAPTER 16

Toren's dragon was a constant presence in his head, a subtle undercurrent to his thoughts, with his own emotions and the occasional dry comment. Usually, that entity was Toren's anchor; when he was feeling angry or anxious, his dragon was a voice of reason and serenity.

Now, it felt like *he* was the steadiness to his dragon's eagerness and yearning.

I'm not going to rush this, he said firmly, and his dragon's impatience and desire nearly swamped him.

Not that his own desire was any less.

And hers wasn't either.

Flushed from their flight, her lips parted, her eyes bright, Toren had never seen anything more beautiful than his mate. He was standing close enough to see her pulse, pounding at her throat, and he wondered if he imagined the sizzle in the air between them.

He didn't imagine Carina's hands, sliding down his chest, down over his hips, and up at last, more centrally located.

The pressure of her fingers gliding over his cock, even

through the fabric of his pants, was almost enough to send Toren over the edge.

Ours, she is ours, his dragon sang joyfully.

"Mine," Carina was saying with equal possessiveness. "You are all mine..."

Toren had to concentrate very hard to make his fingers do something as intricate as unbutton the jacket that Carina was wearing, but then he could slip it off and lay it down on a mossy slope with Carina, who was trying and failing to kiss him and undress him at the same time.

Every part of her that was revealed was a new treasure, a place to kiss and worship, as she wriggled out of her dress and slipped off her tights and pulled helplessly at Toren's shirt as he licked her bare skin and kissed and nibbled.

"Toren..."

"Carina..."

After that the conversation was basically composed of *yeses*, with the occasional ***oh** yes*, and punctuated with hisses and moans of pleasure.

Toren got his shirt off and only lost two of the buttons from the cuffs. Carina's bra was unclipped and tossed aside so that he could put his hands around her perfect breasts and lick her nipples and drag his teeth across her skin as she arched up to him.

He kissed down her tummy to circle around via her thigh and slipped a finger slowly between her folds, releasing the juice that waited there. His tongue followed, lapping carefully as he stroked into her.

Her fingers dug into the moss as she cried out in release of her pleasure and no dragon could have kept Toren back. He tore off his pants, barely not literally, and didn't even bother to remove one of the legs off of his ankle.

Then he was pressing at her entrance, his every plan to go slow and prolong things vanishing in the heat of his desire.

Driven exquisitely by her sounds and the way she rose beneath him, he was reduced to instinct and reaction, following the needs of his nature, and the response of her own.

When she came again, clenching around him, Toren was lost...tumbling off a cliff of pleasure and catching an updraft.

CHAPTER 17

Carina wasn't sure what made her feel more limp, the exhilaration of flying on an honest-to-God *dragon*, the utterly melting after-effects of making love to a gorgeous man who knew exactly how to touch her, or the relief that someone finally knew her whole story and believed her...someone who actually had the power to protect her.

She felt absolutely safe with him.

Illogically safe, she told herself, as they dressed and she despaired of fixing her hair. It was probably part of that *spell*.

They hiked back to the boardwalk, and Carina reminded herself that Amco Bank was powerful. Arguably as powerful as the kingdom of Alaska. Her problems weren't magically over because an Alaskan prince had apparently tripped in a puddle of *true love dust*.

"Let's have lunch at the resort and head back to Fairbanks," Toren suggested, walking hand-in-hand back to the trail with her. "I'll call Rian and get him started on figuring out how to protect you. We can be there for dinner."

Dinner. At the *palace*.

None of it seemed real.

They ate in the main room of the restaurant, at Carina's request. "The private room is so fancy," she said plaintively. "Have some pity on the poor van-dwelling hippy fugitive before you drag her to the palace and make her wear heels and a tiara!"

"A tiara? No, no, it will be a full crown," Toren cautioned her with a wink. "Probably fifty pounds of gold and gems. You'll barely be able to lift your head."

Carina elbowed him, recognizing his teasing.

Toren bought a resort logo sweatshirt to wear instead of his uniform coat, and they only got a few curious stares and second glances; most people looked right past them when they were led to their table.

"Maybe we could run away," he muttered.

Carina was inspecting the menu. "What's that? I'm thinking I need a burger. Are we going to go back out to the pools again before we leave? I'm trying to balance enough food to keep me from fainting again with not so much food that I sink to the bottom."

"Maybe we could run away," Toren repeated, wistfully.

Carina forgot about her menu and gazed up at him. "Really?" she said breathlessly. Then she shook her head. "I doubt you'd be comfortable in my van," she said lightly, as if that was the least of their problems.

"Why not?" Toren asked, looking a little offended.

"Look at you," Carina teased him. "You're looking around for your hot towel right now."

Toren blushed. Their water glasses had been filled twice in the few moments they'd been seated, and the servers were clearly nervous about his foray into the main dining room, but they were doing their best to treat them like any other couple. "I could rough it," he said, adorably defensive and secretly doubtful.

Carina patted him lovingly on the hand. "Of course you

could," she said, like she might say to Shadow. She frowned then, recognizing the cadence in her voice. Shadow had not been near the van when they checked it again, and no one they talked to had seen him.

"Carina..." Toren looked at her anxiously. "You haven't said much about what you left behind. I mean, I'd understand if being queen of Alaska didn't fit your life plans. I honestly don't know what to do about that, but...I'm sorry."

Carina stared at him. "You're apologizing. Because you want me to be a *queen*." She laughed and shook her head helplessly. "I admit that it wasn't even *adjacent* to my original plans. But it definitely beats my own ambitions to make enough at a boring job to afford a house in the suburbs and maybe buy a nice car...and get a dog."

She'd meant it flippantly, but the reminder of Shadow stung.

Toren turned his own hand over and caught hers, stroking her comfortingly.

"I'd put up lost dog posters," Carina said, trying to stuff down her feeling of loss, "but really, he's only been my dog for less than a day. I don't have any real claim on him."

"You loved him," Toren said. "Isn't that a claim?"

His gaze was intense and direct, and Carina had to rein in the irrational joy that bloomed in her.

"*This* isn't love, is it," she said reluctantly. "I mean, you said yourself, it's one of those *magic* things. It's just..." she flapped her free hand helplessly. "Not that you aren't hot, but I usually move a lot slower than this."

"It's not like a *love* spell, exactly," Toren tried to explain. "I mean, magic can't make you *feel* anything. It's just...well, it can *show* you feelings." He looked like he had a mouthful of needles he needed to spit out, then, inconveniently, the server at his elbow cleared his throat.

Carina took her hand back.

Subdued, the two gave their orders.

"I don't know how it is for human mates," Toren said quietly when the server had gone. "I don't even know how it is for dragons, because I need once considered it would happen to me. But I know that you are mine, forever, and that I would never be whole without you."

Carina couldn't answer that, she was such a tangle of longing and it was almost like she was feeling her *own* emotions from a very great distance.

Toren frowned fiercely and for a moment Carina worried that she had inadvertently hurt him. Then she realized with relief that he was frowning past her and she was glad to have something else to say. "Is anything wrong?" she asked.

"Just someone staring at us. Probably nothing." He grinned. "You think I'd be used to it by now."

* * *

AFTER LUNCH, Shadow was waiting by the van, and he greeted them enthusiastically, whining and jumping and wagging his fringed tail. He even threw himself over in the frost-crunchy leaves, wriggling on his back in absolute canine ecstasy.

"Oh, who's a good dog?" Carina asked, scratching at him and kneeling in the leaves to wrestle enthusiastically with him. "Who's the best dog? Who's my *best* Shadow?" It was everything she could do not to cry in happy relief.

Toren greeted him with only a little more decorum, bending to grab him from behind the ears and ruffle his face.

The dog didn't appear to be any worse for the wear after his mysterious adventures.

The van, however...

"Oh my god!" Carina said, sliding the side door open.

The vehicle had been completely tossed. All of her

toiletries had been dumped out on the floor, every food box was out of the cabinet. Even the contents of the fridge had been taken out and left on the bench seat, which had been slashed.

Carina went to the back cabinet, where her tools and clothing were in complete disorder. "They didn't take my money," she said, relief and confusion in her voice.

"They weren't looking for money," Toren said thoughtfully, fingering the cuts in the cushions.

Carina went cold with terror. "The flash drive. They were looking for the flash drive."

"Did you bring it with you?" Toren asked.

She slowly nodded. "I didn't want to leave it with my sister. I made her promise to say that I'd stolen the passport and van once I was gone. I...don't know if she did, but I didn't want to drag her into this. I didn't want to drag *anyone* into this."

"Is it gone?"

Carina drew in a deep breath and glanced around. There were a few people at the far end of the parking lot, exclaiming loudly about a dog mushing display and snapping photos. "Let's find out," she said softly. She took a screwdriver from the tool box and went around to the front of the van.

The driver side headlight cover popped off, revealing a small hollow space beneath the bulb. Carina reached into this and fished out a plastic-wrapped, duct tape-sealed package. She didn't unwrap it, but she did bounce it in her hand thoughtfully before she returned it to its hiding place and replaced the headlight cover.

Carina felt pale with nerves and Toren pulled her into his arms. "They can't hurt you now," he said fiercely. "I won't let them."

She remained stiff and unconsoled. "I should have

switched vehicles in Canada," she said plaintively. "Or... found someone to counterfeit me a new passport or license plates or...I don't know anything about this. I thought I'd gotten far enough away. I thought I'd be safe..."

Toren tipped her chin up to gaze into her eyes. "You *are* safe. They will have to get through me to get you now. Me and the entire kingdom of Alaska, because you are ours now. I don't care how big and powerful and rich the bank is, they don't stand a chance against my brothers and I. We have resources they can't even imagine."

Carina slowly relaxed, and her smile was crooked. "And dragons. Don't forget, you're dragons."

Toren kissed her forehead. "We'll protect you," he said confidently. "*I'll* protect you."

She took a shaky breath. "This is really not what I thought my life would look like a few weeks ago. The most exciting thing in my future was the possibility of a promotion."

"Me neither," Toren confessed. "Last week, I was hunting caribou on the North Slope, no thoughts about the future beyond the vague idea that things would be freezing up for hockey soon. This week, I'm staring at a throne. It's..."

"...crazy?" Carina finished for him.

"Crazy," Toren agreed. "And a little terrifying. But Carina...Carina, my love, I wouldn't trade it for anything if it meant not having you. I could face anything with you at my side."

She sighed into him, not wanting to admit how completely and foolishly she trusted him. "What now?" she asked plaintively.

"Fairbanks," Toren said. "Let's get your van tidied up and go to Fairbanks. We can talk to my brothers. They'll know what to do."

They straightened up the van and Carina patched the cushions with duct tape.

Shadow remained underfoot for the entire process; he clearly had no intention of being lost again. Carina put his new collar on him, and he immediately sat down and tried to scratch beneath it.

When Toren went to sit in the passenger seat, he found that the dog had already claimed the seat. "Move over," he told the grinning hound.

Shadow reluctantly gave up the chair and sat between them until Carina started the vehicle. Then he climbed into Toren's lap to watch out the window. Toren laughingly let him stay there as they drove away from the resort.

CHAPTER 18

Carina's van was under-powered and drove like a box of nails, rattling loudly over potholes and frost-heaves. But Toren had to admit that there was something freeing and *fun* about hitting the open road with a large dog monopolizing his lap and Carina sitting so close that he could reach out and touch her any time he wanted to.

He could feel some of the tension leaching from her as they left the resort gates behind them. The road was a safe place, for her, and he wondered if his presence gave her any of the same irresistible contentment that hers gave him.

"I have questions," she said, after a few miles.

"I will answer anything I can," he replied, scratching Shadow's ears.

"I hardly know where to start," Carina admitted, setting the cruise control. "So, there's dragons and magic in Alaska, which doesn't somehow surprise me as much as it should. Are there other dragons? Is everyone in the whole kingdom a dragon shifter?"

"Only the royal family," Toren answered. "Er, all the royal families in the Small Kingdoms."

Carina chewed on that in silence for a moment, while Toren tried to decide if he should elaborate at all. They came around a curve in the road where bright sunlight was suddenly sharp in their faces because of the low angle of the sun. Carina winced and put the visor down.

"Who knows?" she asked. "Is it a big secret, or am I just especially oblivious?"

"I don't know how it works in every kingdom, but it's a pretty close secret here. Immediate castle staff knows, and some members of the elected council. Some of them are other kinds of shifters themselves."

"Other kinds? There are other kinds of shifters?" Carina glanced at him in alarm. "Like unicorns and firebirds?"

"I've never met a unicorn or a firebird," Toren said, adjusting Shadow on his lap so that the dog's elbows weren't digging into his leg. "But there are *normal* animal shifters. The captain of our guard is a polar bear shifter. One of our regular housekeepers is an otter shifter."

"And is *that* a secret?"

"In most places, yes. I mean, except on a few of the more isolated islands, people aren't out there just shifting around in public. It's something your family usually knows, because it's usually passed to children, and maybe a close friend or two."

"But just in the Small Kingdoms?"

Toren shook his head. "All over the world. In the United States, too. They just keep their heads down and stay in the shadows."

"Werewolves," Carina said wonderingly.

"Misdirection may be used on occasion," Toren warned. "Most of the big media outlets are run by shifters, so they have reason to keep the movies splashy and the real news quiet."

"Makes sense," Carina agreed, though Toren could feel the rumbling disquiet of her worldview resettling.

After a moment, she asked, "So...magic. Can all shifters do magic?"

Toren hesitated, then explained, "All shifters *are* magic. But not all shifters *do* magic. And some non-shifters can do magic, too."

"So you don't *do* magic to change shape?"

Toren had never had to describe the rules of magic before, and it was harder than he'd guessed. "My brother, Raval, he'd be able to clarify this better than I can, but there's natural magic, and there's *structured* magic. Natural magic is what shifters have. We can move between two forms, and there's the cloaking to keep people from noticing us. It's all very innate and informal; you just think about it, and there you go."

"So, what about the other kind?" Carina asked.

"The other kind?"

"You said there were two kinds, natural and...*not* natural?"

"Structured." Toren laughed despite himself. "Okay, so some people—I'm not one of them—can basically use natural magic to do...er, things. They have to write the words out, very specifically."

"Like, a spell? There are *wizards*?"

"Except that it's not a poem or Latin or whatever. They have to write down what the magic is supposed to do, and it does it. The kingdoms have this...pact."

"Even I've heard of the Compact," Carina said. The road had turned again, and she put up the visor.

"You've heard of the *public* version of the Compact," Toren clarified. "That one lays out trade agreements and stuff." Toren was keenly aware that he was out of his depth for this explanation, as well. Fask generally kept tabs on that kind of thing.

"But the private version is a lot longer, and stickier, and has a lot of rules about magic and succession. For example, it doesn't just *say* that we can't use magic against one another, it actually *stops us* from using magic against one another; spells we cast against each other would backfire terribly. The Compact itself is generally accepted to be the most complicated spell in existence. It protects the kingdoms from using magic against each other, and it...picks the succession of each kingdom."

"By magic," Carina said flatly. "This *mate* thing."

"Right," Toren said, gazing at her profile. His mate. His destined partner. "It makes sure that we meet, and that we know each other when we do."

She was silent, frowning forward at the road, then cast a sideways glance at him. "Destiny," she said softly. She didn't feel entirely happy about it.

Shadow was getting restless in his lap and Toren snapped his fingers to draw him off. The big dog walked to the back bench of the van, then returned to sit between them and finally lie down.

Carina mused, "It's kind of hard to wrap my head around this spell idea. You just write it down? Like in a notebook?"

"Spells on paper only work once; there's too much power and it burns up. You can also anchor the structured magic into an object. Like a rock. Or a jewel. Or the Compact itself, I guess. Or a piece of metal. But of course, it's harder to write on those things."

"Like a magic sword?"

"Sort of. It wouldn't be like a sentient weapon that talks to you or anything, but it could have special properties. There's an obsidian dagger in my father's hoard that is spelled to kill any dragon with just a scratch. Moose!"

"It will kill a moose?" Carina asked in confusion.

Toren pointed. "No, there's a moose!"

CHAPTER 19

Carina stomped on the brakes. The moose at the edge of the road, his broad antlers dripping with strips of velvet, chose that moment to cross.

He was a magnificent animal, nearly as tall as her van, and he gave Carina a baleful glance from one beady eye as he sauntered in front of her.

Shadow whined, dancing between the seats and bouncing in place to see out of the front window. His tail wagged furiously.

"Wow," Carina said, watching the moose pause at the side of the road to strip the tips off a stand of willow. "What a beast."

Shadow tried to climb into her lap for a better view out the side window and Carina pushed him off. "He doesn't want to play, Shadow."

Something occurred to her. "If there are people running around in animal form, how do you know if you're looking at a regular animal or a shifter?"

"A shifter is smart enough not to run around in animal

form during hunting season, usually," Toren pointed out. "And knows better than to cross the road in front of traffic."

"They don't have...like a secret handshake or something?" Carina eased off the brakes again as the moose wandered back into the forest and disappeared. For such a large creature, he was invisible almost at once.

Toren chuckled. "Not to my knowledge."

Carina put the van in motion again. Shadow gave a suffering sigh and sat down, putting his head in her lap. They drove in silence for a while, Carina trying to sort out all the things that Toren had told her. Magic. Shifters. Succession. *Queen of Alaska*. She caught herself slowing the van down as her brain swirled reluctantly. She reset the cruise control so that she wouldn't slow to a crawl.

"Your family..."

"They're going to love you," Toren said, as if he could guess at the nervous spiral of her thoughts.

Carina wasn't convinced. She had no illusions that the quality of her character in any way balanced the baggage of her recent past.

She had to take the van out of cruise control as they got closer to Fairbanks and there was suddenly traffic again. From lots of nothing, there were suddenly houses again: first lone dwellings barely visible down long driveways, then more and more of them until they were abruptly in Fairbanks.

Fairbanks was barely large enough to call a city. Even the so-called downtown had only a few buildings more than three or four stories, and the tallest looked smaller than fifteen stories. Compared to Portland, it was downright puny. But it was a pretty city. The buildings, as Carina skirted the city, were a mix of dated architecture and newer structures. Many of them had colorful murals. Toren directed her along the bank of the river, which was traced with a wide recreation path and edged by a wrought iron fence.

There were trees everywhere, even right downtown: big, dark spruce trees and birch trees in autumn colors, plus shorter ornamental trees hung with red leaves and dark berries.

The palace was nestled into the side of a hill, several sprawling wings of it just visible over the forest it was settled into. It grew larger every time Carina saw it through the trees. Houses and business fell away behind them and the final approach was through a gate—they were waved through—down a long, private driveway through wild-looking forest that opened onto a huge yard. She pulled to the bottom of wide steps leading up to massive front doors with big glass panels. *Did they build the entire castle to dragon scale?* Carina wondered in awe.

Then those great doors were opening, and Carina was sorely tempted to slam on the gas and follow the driveway around and back out the way they'd come in.

CHAPTER 20

Toren hadn't been particularly detailed on the phone when he called Fask to let his brothers know that he was bringing a mate home. He'd given them the barest skeleton version of Carina's troubles, and her full name, so that Fask and Rian could begin investigating...and very little else.

He knew they must be wild with curiosity, not sure what to expect. He could feel Carina's nervousness, fluttering like a panicked bird in her stomach. His new world and his old were about to collide.

Shadow was getting agitated in the stopped van, sure that this meant he could get out and confused about why he wasn't. He climbed into Toren's lap and put his nose on the window, panting in excitement. Carina reached back and found his leash, clipping it firmly onto the collar. Toren took the lead.

The door to the van squeaked open as a casually-dressed member of the castle staff came forward to assist. At the slightest gap, Shadow was bolting out, and only dragon strength kept him back as Toren scrambled out after him.

"You'd be a good wheel dog," Toren chuckled. "You're stronger than you look."

Carina came around and hesitantly gave her van keys to the man with a glance for confirmation at Toren. "I don't think this old thing has once in its life been parked by a valet," she observed. She took Shadow's leash from Toren, and Shadow, his ears swiveling and his tail wagging low, immediately attempted to circle around them both.

Toren wasn't quite fast enough to step out of the leash before it had wrapped around his legs, and Carina's, and they had to cling to each other for balance as Carina desperately said, "Shadow, no! Don't! Wrong way!" and tried to untangle them.

Shadow whined in mad, trapped panic and tried to lunge away, until Carina bodily tackled him, dragging Toren with her.

"It's okay, boy. It's okay." Carina had a solid hold on the big dog. Toren was able to unclip the leash, unwind it from around them, and clip it back on.

Carina brushed off her knees and straightened her flannel over-shirt. "That was not the first impression I was going for," she admitted in a stage whisper.

Shadow leaned against her legs and panted, but stepped forward when they went forward to meet the three men who were coming down the steps. The big dog gave a belated impression of a well-behaved dog...until they arrived at the bottom of the stairs, where he lifted his leg and peed briefly on a statue of an important-looking man.

If Carina had looked embarrassed before, it was mortification on her face now. "I'm so sorry," she managed weakly. To her credit, she kept her chin up as she faced down Toren's brothers. Toren slipped his hand into hers and she squeezed it.

"Nice dog," Tray said.

"Welcome," Fask said.

Rian didn't say anything, but his nod was polite.

"This is Carina," Toren said, wishing he'd practiced this part. "She's...she's my mate."

He wasn't sure if Carina's squeeze was out of new terror or if she was trying to give him courage. Either way, he held on so tightly he was surprised either of them had feeling in their fingers.

There was a moment of quiet as everyone present was reminded of the significance of the statement, then Fask stepped forward and extended his hand. "We're happy to have you here," he said sincerely. "Please make yourself at home."

"I'm afraid that Mrs. James isn't going to want the dog inside," Rian pointed out, after taking his turn at shaking Carina's hand.

"He can go hang out in the kennel, can't he," Tray suggested, coming forward to greet Shadow as enthusiastically as he greeted Carina. "Who's a good dog? I've always hated that statue, too." He stood up and offered his hand for the leash. "I'll take him if you want. I promise he'll be well cared for."

Carina hesitated, then quipped, "I never did ask what dragons eat," and everyone froze again.

After a breath of surprise, Tray gave an un-princely snort of humor, Fask grinned, and even Rian cracked a smile.

"Burgers, mostly," Tray assured her. "Thai food. I'm Tray. I'm the good-looking twin."

"I like wild caribou," Fask said. Then he smiled and added, "But I like it grilled, or cooked into sausage best. Fask. I'm the oldest."

"Bossiest," coughed Tray with a wink at Carina.

"The only dogs I eat are hot dogs," Rian said, straight-faced. "Call me Rian."

They parted to lead Carina into the castle as Toren gave Tray the leash for Shadow and she petted him and said goodbye.

Some of Toren's nervousness evaporated. They were going to accept Carina; they knew that she'd be a perfect queen, just like he did.

Then he remembered that this meant he was going to be king, and all the nervousness came rushing back and he wished he'd pushed harder for running away. Maybe they could have gotten lost in Canada.

Carina's awe when they walked in made Toren take an appraising look at the castle. Past a big arctic entryway, sweeping stairs went up to the second floor.

A chandelier four times the size of her van glittered from the high ceiling over the foyer. Everything was done in Art Nouveau style, with long, sweeping lines everywhere. His grandfather, lacking anything resembling subtlety, had commissioned the returns of the stair railings to be dragons, leaping to the ground, their wings tucked to their backs. The downstairs foyer was practically an art gallery, with choice pieces of art hanging on the walls, mostly Impressionist and Renaissance paintings, but also a selection of Sydney Laurence's most famous Alaskan landscapes and a wide array of Native Alaskan masks.

"We do most of our entertaining at the hot springs," Fask explained as he led them further in. "The palace is set up much more as a home then a hotel. But we've got plenty of extra rooms, and I hope you'll be comfortable here."

"Some home," Carina observed breathlessly, craning her head to see the great beams of the ceiling above.

Most of the central structure was stone, but the floors were polished wood, and there were natural log columns at each side, leading the way to the wings. The architect had apparently thought that Alaska meant log cabins, and the wings were all rich, warm log wood on the interior. The natural wood grain made up most of the visual interest, and lace curtains framed big windows that looked out on birch and spruce forest. The upper floors had views of the mountains to the south.

The Art Nouveau theme followed them into the log wings, and there were wrought iron handles in graceful shapes on everything. A large, glass-fronted fireplace insert gave a wide view of the flickering fire within.

Across the top of the fireplace, stylized metal salmon were leaping, and the metal art continued around the room, stark black against the sunny wood; there were moose browsing at waving willows, with wolves howling in the distance. The furniture in the study was all comfortable, wood and leather, with more black iron accents. Thick, plush rugs covered the wood floor here.

Toren had never really appreciated any of it; it had always struck him as tacky, over-the-top, Alaskan-to-the-max. But Carina, as they ushered her into the study, gazed around like she'd never seen anything like it, and she clearly loved it.

"May I take your coat?" Rian asked. He kept trying to meet Toren's eyes over Carina's, but Toren was too busy watching Carina drink in all the new sights, reveling in the delight and awe she was feeling.

"We've had a room made up for you," Fask said kindly, taking her insulated flannel shirt from Rian as if it were the finest fur coat. "I hope you'll be very comfortable here. Let me have Mrs. James make us some refreshment."

He vanished, while Rian settled into one of the leather chairs. Toren drew Carina down beside him on the loveseat. She sat very primly, smoothing her jumper over her knees, and he could feel the nervousness rippling through her.

"So, Carina," Rian started. "I understand you're wanted for murder?"

CHAPTER 21

Carina was saved having to answer by the return of Tray, who flopped into a chair opposite from them. "Shadow has been fed and given a lovely house full of straw and I promise that no one has eaten him," he said, laughing. He was wearing a bright blue hockey jersey for the Alaska team and Carina found him an odd foil to Rian; the two were identical and yet very definitely distinct. Rian looked like a gruff librarian, Tray looked like someone who got caught hamming it up on the sports audience camera frequently.

"Thank you," Carina murmured. She reminded herself that Shadow was not actually her dog and that she should take him to Fairbanks to get checked for a chip and compared against lost dog reports. Toren squeezed her hand as if he'd felt her sudden grief at the thought of giving him up. Probably he had. The idea was both deeply unsettling and somehow comforting.

Fask returned with a tall woman in a sharp uniform carrying a sheaf of papers. "Captain Luke has been checking into the accusations," he said, as they both took seats across from Toren and Carina.

Captain Luke was a beautiful, ageless Native Alaskan woman with a round, warm-skinned face who looked like she could twist Carina into a pretzel without trying. Dark hair was pulled back in a neat bun, and she had three dark lines tattooed down her chin.

Carina tried not to stare at them.

"We've confirmed that there is a warrant out for your arrest," the captain said smoothly. "For murder in the first degree, automobile theft, identity theft, and corporate espionage."

"I never did any corporate espionage!" Carina protested. Then she heard her own words and had to laugh dryly. "Or the murder, of course."

"Of course," Fask said, without a trace of humor. Carina supposed she should be glad that he seemed to believe her.

"My sister?" She was almost afraid to ask.

"Your sister appears to be unharmed," the captain said reassuringly. "We haven't tried to make contact yet, in case she's being observed."

"We'd like to hear your account of the events," Fask said.

His voice wasn't unkind, Carina thought, and she could feel the supportive warmth of Toren at her side as she drew in a breath. "I was working for an accounting firm in Portland," she began. She told them the story as dispassionately as she could manage, from the discovery of the data to her flight out of the country.

They all listened grimly, nodding and asking questions, and no one implied that she'd been an idiot for not trusting the police to protect her or trying to go public without more support.

"I didn't really know what I'd do when I got here," she confessed. "I guess I hoped that I could just stay low, regroup, and find someone who was willing to help me find justice."

"What made you choose Alaska?" Captain Luke asked shortly.

Carina tried to convince herself it didn't sound accusing. "I could drive here," she said. "And, no offense, but Alaska still has this reputation of being the kind of place you could go to a bar and throw darts at your own wanted poster."

That earned her a ripple of laughter, and the captain seemed to relax a fraction.

Someone cleared their voice from the doorway and Carina look around to find a figure who must clearly be Mrs. James. She was a stout-looking woman of indeterminate age with brunette hair in a practical bob.

She circled the room, handing each of them a drink. Carina smelled coffee and chocolate, but her own cup was a tea of a gorgeous pink color in a clear mug.

"Wild rosehip, rose petals, lowbush cranberry, dried lemon peel, hibiscus, and a little honey. Some of these fools drink coffee this late, but I thought you could use something a little easier on the nerves after the day you've had." Her dark eyes were kind and gentle and Carina gave her a cautious smile as she took the hot cup.

Carina took a careful sip, and it was as bright and delicious as it looked. "I didn't realize it was so late," she admitted. It had taken some time to drive to Fairbanks from Angel Hot Springs, and their lunch had been ages ago. Outside the windows, the forest had turned twilight blue, though it was still plenty bright enough to see by.

"Some of the questions can surely wait until morning," Mrs. James said, with a meaningful look at Fask and at the captain.

"Of course, Mrs. James," Fask acquiesced immediately.

Captain Luke stood and bowed crisply. "I will check the security of the van and see to the attachment of a guard to

Ms. Andresen." She left at Fask's nod, not even glancing at Toren.

Mrs. James cheerfully said, "I've had Felix prepare a light meal to be served in forty-five minutes. Miss Andresen, your room has been made up and if you'd like to bring your cup, I can show you where you'll be staying and give you a chance to freshen up."

Carina scrambled to her feet, nearly spilling her tea in her haste, and everyone else stood politely. Was Mrs. James implying that she *should* freshen up? The castle was magnificent, but everyone was dressed reassuringly casually.

She took a hasty gulp of her drink so it wasn't so full, and shot Toren a longing look; he was her anchor in this whole crazy, upside down world. His look in return was just as desperate, but he let her fingers slip from his without protest.

A queen, she reminded herself, feeling dizzy. She should at least try to act like one.

So she drew in a deep breath and followed Mrs. James, concentrating on keeping her chin high and her tea *inside* the cup.

CHAPTER 22

Once Carina was gone, Toren felt everyone's attention shift as they settled back into their seats.

His cup, full of hot chocolate because Mrs. James still insisted on treating him like a wayward child (and also because he continued to request it), was suddenly very interesting.

The whole dynamic in the room was new and different.

It wasn't just that everyone was looking at him; that frequently happened when he said something dumb, or when he was in trouble for shirking tutors or duties.

It was that everyone was looking at him *thoughtfully*.

All of sudden, he'd gone from the *screw-up youngest brother* to *going-to-be-king*, whether any of them liked it or not.

"So," Tray said archly. "*Car-ee-na.*"

Toren made the mistake of looking up from his foamy cocoa.

Tray was leering suggestively, and Toren had a sudden primal urge to punch him.

Our mate's honor, his dragon rumbled.

"She seems clever enough," Fask said peacefully, giving

Tray a quelling look. "And she's lovely. I think she'll appeal to the people, and we'll be able to come out on top of this little drama."

"I didn't mean to," Toren said, feeling very young and stupid.

"Mean to what?" Fask asked sharply.

"Find my mate. I mean, everyone wants you to be king. I didn't want this. Not that I don't want *her*, I..." Toren put his cocoa down on an end table more firmly than he meant to and a little splashed over the side.

"I can't be sorry for it," he said softly, meeting Fask's gaze. "I feel like I ought to apologize, and I'd give this to you if I could. Not her, I could never give her up. I'm... oh, lights," he groaned, slumping back in his seat. "I'm not saying any of this right. I'm going to be the stupidest king in the history of the Small Kingdoms and Alaska will be the laughingstock of the Compact."

Kind laughter answered him.

"Poor kid," Tray drawled, reaching over to ruffle Toren's head.

Toren batted him away in irritation. "I have a real problem here," Toren protested. "The Compact has clearly made a terrible mistake," Something occurred to him. "Can I give the crown to someone else after the Renewal?"

Fask frowned. "Leave him alone, Tray," he said. "You can't really take away the crown once it's in place. Not without another king to pass it to."

"Maybe father will wake up," Rian suggested. "I mean, it's still possible that he's just going to come around."

"We can all hope so," Tray muttered.

"I'm still studying the Compact for a way around this," Rian said. "Interestingly, there's a woman at the University of Florida who was doing a thesis on the Compact. It looks like the library there had an unaltered copy of the Compact."

That took all the attention away from Toren at least.

"Unaltered?" Fask repeated in alarm.

Copies of the uncensored Compact were kept under strict lock and key. That someone in a human nation had a copy of such a thing was alarming to say the least.

"*Had*," Rian repeated. "Small Kingdom agents replaced it last year. The thesis hasn't been finished. But the public prospectus had some *very* interesting theories and fresh insights. I'm going to be getting in contact with the student, see if I can pick her brain about some of the things she must have seen."

Fask frowned. "Tread carefully," he advised. "The last thing we need is an exposé to cover up."

"I've got a good feeling about this," Rian said.

Toren looked at him dubiously. Rian didn't usually run on feelings. He was always the logical one, looking for proof, reasons, and hard data.

Fask still looked concerned. "If she's got too much information, she may need to be silenced," he cautioned.

Everyone looked at him.

"Not like that," Fask protested. "Geez, you guys. I meant that we might have to hire someone to hack in and delete the thesis prospectus from the university database and pay her off."

Toren wondered if these were the kinds of decisions that he was going to be expected to make. It wouldn't have occurred to him that someone's *thesis* might endanger their greatest secrets. Shouldn't a king have thought of that?

"In the meantime," Fask said impatiently, "we've got a name to clear and a wedding to plan."

Toren looked at him blankly until he realized that Fask meant *his* wedding. His wedding to Carina. They were all looking at *him* again.

"I suppose a quiet courthouse wedding is going to be out of the question?" Toren attempted a laugh.

"Do you really think that the people are going to let the first royal wedding in sixty years happen at a courthouse?" Fask asked. "No, we're going to have to go all out."

"We'll have to invite royalty from the other Small Kingdoms," Rian said thoughtfully.

"And diplomats from the United States, probably," Kenth suggested. "Does she have a big family?"

"I have no idea," Toren whispered, suddenly as horrified by the prospect of a giant wedding as he was of being king. "I haven't technically asked her to marry me yet." Panic washed over him. "What if she says no?"

Everyone laughed, which did nothing to soothe Toren's ruffled nerves.

"I'll get working with the guard and our lawyers to figure out how we're going to clear Carina and I'll hire an event coordinator," Fask said, because Fask knew how to get things done. "Your job, your *only* job right now, is to get your mate to marry you."

"Even Toren ought to be able to handle that," Tray said, standing. "I smell food, and I want to wash up before dinner."

Everyone else rose as well, and Toren drifted along behind them in a daze.

Everything was happening so fast that he had no idea what to do or how to do it.

And the further in he got, the more Toren wished that he and Carina really had run away.

CHAPTER 23

Mrs. James was not even slightly subtle as she showed Carina where Toren's rooms were, just down the hallway and around a corner from the third story apartment that had been prepared for her.

"There's not a lot of traffic in these halls after bedtime," Mrs. James assured her, face serene. "But there are sometimes spirits. They won't hurt you."

Carina had no idea if she was teasing or not and glanced sideways to see if there were clues on her face.

That was when she noticed the two guards following discreetly behind them.

Then Mrs. James opened the doors into her room, and any suspicion that she was being mocked vanished into astonishment.

The walls here were polished log, and the big, triple-paned windows were hung with lacy curtains. There was just enough light left in the sky to see the range, huge and distant and blue, edging the horizon over the tops of dark evergreens.

"Wow," she said. But the view was the least of the room's features.

A giant four-poster bed was against one wall, an entire sitting room with couches and a desk against the other, and an open door suggested a giant private bathroom. Tall, ornate wardrobes were bolted to the walls.

There were clothes laid out at the foot of the bed.

"I'm... ah... thank you," she said.

"The clothing won't fit terribly well, I'm afraid," Mrs. James said apologetically. "We have an excess of men's clothing in all sizes, but for women's sizes, it's just my closet and the housekeeper's." She didn't suggest raiding Captain Luke's closet, but Carina privately wondered if the captain had any clothing that wasn't a uniform.

The clothing was not the fancy ballgowns that Carina had been half-hoping for and half-dreading. There were two knee-length skirts, a few blouses, a white sweater, and a pair of stretchy leggings. There was no underwear, and there was one package of black men's socks. "I do have some clothes at the van," she said. "But this looks great. Thank you so much, Mrs...ah..."

"You may call me Julia," the woman said kindly. "But the boys may not." She gave Carina a wink. "They won't take me seriously if I don't maintain boundaries."

"You're the...housekeeper?" Carina guessed, not wanting to assume.

"Close enough," Julia said. "I've been with the family since Fask was young, and when they didn't need a nanny any longer, I stayed to make sure they didn't get into trouble. The boys are good about doing their own chores, so we don't have a lot of full time staff. I'll be sure to introduce you around tomorrow."

She smiled at Carina kindly. "We'll have some formalwear made for you, but this is Alaska. No one will blink if you want to wear jeans and flannel most of the time. We can sit down together and put together an on-line order, or I can send you with a driver to do some shopping downtown, whichever you'd prefer. Or, if you'd like a road trip, Anchorage has a wider selection. We can arrange a flight or a drive if you'd like to see the sights. There isn't snow in the forecast yet, so it would be a scenic trip."

"That would be amazing, thank you," Carina squeaked.

She led Carina into the bathroom. "All the standard amenities. If there are any brands you prefer, please leave a note and I'll have it stocked. Extra towels are here; there's a bathrobe behind the door."

They returned to the main room. "If there's anything you need, please don't hesitate to ask. Dinner will be in about thirty-five minutes, down one flight and to the right for the informal dining hall."

"Thank you," Carina murmured, because she ought to say something, even if she'd already said *thank you* so many times it was starting to lose meaning.

Julia paused in the doorway. "We're all glad to have you here," she said warmly. "If those boys give you any trouble, just threaten to tell Mrs. James. Toren's a sweet lad, and I'm happy for both of you."

Then, with a twinkling smile, she was shutting the door and Carina was alone.

Not wanting to squander her time before dinner, Carina took a brief, luxurious shower. She gave the bathtub a wistful look, but that would wait.

She dried off briskly, and put on the leggings under one of the skirts. They were a little bit short, but at least they covered her legs. She picked a maroon blouse that mostly matched the skirt, and put the sweater over it. Men's socks and her worn hiking boots completed the image.

It was definitely...not royal looking. But it was clean,

comfortable, and warm, which was more than Carina had been able to say for a while.

She towel-dried her hair and combed through it, then drew in her breath, gathered her courage, and left the room.

She was not surprised to find the two guards waiting there.

"I'm just...ah...going to dinner," she said shyly to them.

"Yes, my lady," one of them said, just as the other said, "Yes, ma'am." They gave each other startled looks.

They didn't know what to call her, either, Carina realized.

For some reason that was a great comfort. She mentally named them Grim and Amused for their original expressions.

She walked down the hall and drew up at Toren's door. Was he even there? Should they arrive together, or was she expected to make an entrance by herself?

As she was still considering whether to knock, keenly aware of the guards watching her with their bland faces, the door burst open.

"Oh, Carina," Toren said, and then he was sweeping her into his arms and everything was as it should be again. She had to remind herself that this was just a magic spell because it felt so safe and wonderful in his embrace.

"We should have run away when you first suggested it," Carina whispered. "I bet we could be in Canada by now."

"Everyone is being nice to you, aren't they?" Toren demanded, putting her down and giving the guards a fierce look over her shoulder.

"Yes, everyone is wonderful, I shouldn't complain," Carina said quietly, hoping she didn't sound ungrateful. She could feel all the tension, trembling inside of her.

Toren gave her one chaste kiss on the cheek and whispered in her ear, "We should grab Shadow and make a break for it now..."

Carina's stomach growled audibly. "Maybe after dinner?" she suggested with a giggle. She could do this. She could keep it together a little longer. That was how she'd gotten this far, just taking it moment by moment, step by step.

The whole castle smelled amazing, and it only got stronger as Toren took her arm and led her down one flight of stairs.

Clinging to one another, they sailed into a dining room that Carina would never in a million years have called informal, and were led to side-by-side seats near the head of the table. The chair at the end was empty, though a place was set.

"You're moving up, little brother," Tray said, elbowing him in the side.

"You're not going to be able to call me that when I'm king," Toren hissed back.

"You will always be our little brother," Tray teased.

Everyone sat at once when Fask, across the table from them, gestured, and Carina followed suit.

The meal itself was surprisingly casual; everyone passed dishes around and served themselves. There were no extra forks to wonder about. There were chicken legs, noodles tossed in pesto sauce, small red potatoes and gravy, green beans, sliced tomatoes, and hot biscuits. Carina wasn't sure what she'd been expecting, but it felt surprisingly homey and comfortable.

"Your timing is good," Fask told her from across the table. "This is all local produce, including the basil in the pesto. A few months from now, all of our fresh vegetables will have to be shipped in, and the quality declines sharply."

"There are downsides to being at the ass end of the supply chain," Tray said. "Ouch! I can say ass." He glared at Rian, who had apparently kicked him.

Rian muttered something Carina couldn't quite hear about *being* an ass.

She was introduced to Raval, the blond brother that she remembered was the one who worked in structured magic. He didn't seem much like a wizard, but he was quiet among the chaos of his brothers.

Gradually, Carina began to relax.

This wasn't the state meal she had expected, or the snooty air. These were brothers, teasing each other and tossing biscuits down the table, and they were kindly trying to include her and put her at ease. They asked about her life in careful ways, skirting the topic of murder accusations and corporate espionage.

To her surprise, they whole-heartedly approved of her living in her van.

"Those old VWs are really cool," Fask said enthusiastically. "They can go places a lot of modern RVs wouldn't fit."

"Like logging trails and royal land," Rian said, with a friendly wink at Carina.

"Did you really think you could stay all winter there?" Tray asked around a very un-princely mouthful of food.

"I hoped I wouldn't have to," Carina said. "It has a propane heater, and I have two sleeping bags and long underwear. But to be honest, I'm just as happy I don't have to test the theory that I *could*."

"It'll definitely be warmer in Toren's bed," Tray said, nodding wisely.

Toren blushed, adorably, and Carina had to giggle.

Her laughter died on her lips as she remembered that it was just a magic spell, it wasn't really love.

CHAPTER 24

After dinner, their dishes were quietly removed and their water glasses were refilled. Toren found himself the unwelcome center of attention again. At least this time Carina was at his side. He could feel her unease, but he wasn't sure what was causing it. There was a lot to choose from.

"Let's talk about timing," Fask said mildly. "We need to host an engagement party, then there's the actual marriage, and a coronation. We don't want to stack these all up on top of each other."

"People might think we hurried the wedding to cover the pregnancy," Tray said slyly and Carina choked on the water she was drinking.

"I'm not—!" She seemed to realize that Tray was teasing her and glowered at him.

If he had been in reach, Toren would have punched his brother.

"On that topic..." Fask started gravely, and Toren sputtered in protest.

"I have an IUD," Carina said firmly. Her cheeks were scarlet, but her chin was high. "And I have no plans to remove it soon. Can we please tackle one crazy life-changing event at a time?"

"You don't have to get that personal," Toren growled. He wondered if it would be too obvious if he took her hand. It had been easier—or at least less complicated—to save her from drowning than to save her from his siblings.

"We actually do, little brother," Tray said. "The whole point of a king having a mate is that the line continues."

"We don't know that," Rian argued. "The Compact never mentions children."

"At any rate, it can wait," Fask said quellingly. "I apologize for making you uncomfortable, Carina. What can't wait is the engagement party. If we want this to look like a natural progression, that should be soon."

"And the murder accusation?" Rian reminded them.

"That makes everything quite tricky," Fask confirmed. "It's going to take time to clear charges like that. I'll arrange a meeting with the bank's executives and see if I can't start a negotiation. We should try to have the engagement party immediately; we want to make sure that our claim on Carina is established. I think we should time it for the diplomatic visit from the Mo'orea king and queen next weekend."

Our claim, Toren's dragon snarled. *Not his.*

Toren wrestled him back. "What are you going to negotiate?"

"We can offer to destroy the flash drive if they make the charges disappear."

"You want to just let them get away with it?" Carina cried in outrage, cutting across their conversation. "They laundered billions of dollars and murdered some poor woman! That's *bullshit* and I won't be a part of it!"

"Proving any of that will be exceedingly difficult," Fask said warningly. "They have resources beyond even ours, the best lawyers, and they clearly aren't afraid to dirty their hands to cover their own tracks. They've killed once and they've probably done an admirable job of scrubbing the evidence from their own systems by this point. The only thing we have is one flash drive that may or may not prove something that it's going to be hard to pin on any one person. Justice would be the hard road, and it would take time we don't have. Years, probably. Years you could spend in prison, I should point out."

"Then it takes years," Carina snarled. "It takes years and it's done right, or I'll walk now. I'm not going to let her die in vain, and I'm not going to take a *crown* in return for my silence."

Toren, familiar with his brother's expressions, watched him wrestle with several emotions and settle on grudging respect.

"Spoken like a true queen of Alaska," Fask said at last.

"Can we keep her?" Tray asked lightly.

Carina's knuckles were white on the arms of her chair. Toren ached to take her into his arms, but didn't want to undermine her show of strength.

Fask was shaking his head. "I respect your decision to take the high road, my lady, but we still need a way to protect you if America requests extradition."

"Can't we just give her asylum?" Tray asked.

"Framed for murder isn't one of the protected grounds for persecution," Rian said.

Everyone looked at him blankly.

Patiently, Rian explained, "She can appeal for asylum, but we have policies that we have to apply and Alaska can only grant asylum if the applicant can prove that they would be unfairly persecuted by their *government* for reasons of race, political opinion, religion, or nationality. If she committed a crime—is suspected of a crime—then she has to stand trial for that crime." He gave Carina an apologetic shrug. "Even if we believe you didn't commit it."

"Give her a new identity?" Tray suggested.

Carina made a noise of protest.

Rian shook his head. "I don't think we'd be capable of giving her a new identity that would defeat the celebrity columns and Internet busybodies."

"Or the deep pockets of Amco Bank," Fask said thoughtfully. "They clearly already know that she's here."

"A fake identity could also negate some terms in the Compact," Rian cautioned. "There are a lot of specifics in there regarding falsehood and deceit."

"No new identity," Fask said firmly. "Rian, talk to our lawyer and see if you can find any loopholes in the asylum rules."

"Maybe they just won't ask for extradition?" Toren hazarded.

Tray snorted. "I'm guessing Fask wasn't thinking about a secret engagement party. She's going to be spread out across every glossy gossip magazine and all across the Internet. It won't take any sleuthing at all to know she's here."

Toren gathered his courage. He didn't usually make suggestions during these meetings, but he wasn't going to sit things out with Carina at stake. "Yeah, but will they really *ask us* to extradite the crown princess of Alaska? With all the negative publicity and political tensions it would cause? Let's go as big as possible. They're going to dig up her warrant, that information is public record, right? So come out in front of it, tell the truth. Say she's here in fear of her life, that she was framed, that she's afraid to leave...that we fell in love. People will eat it up with a spoon. The US won't *want* to ask for her. Not without a fair, public trial. And Amco Bank doesn't want that if Carina's got evidence, so *they're* going to stall, and we can take the time we need to figure out how to bring them down."

They all stared at him with various expressions of concern, doubt, and surprise.

Carina reached over and took his hand, smiling at him, and that was the only look that mattered.

"Are you seriously suggesting that we try to bluff the United States out of asking us to hand over a wanted criminal?" Tray asked.

"For a little while, at least," Toren said faintly.

"Ballsy," Raval said approvingly.

Fask looked darkly worried. "I'd want the details kept quiet," he said. "Say it's classified. Don't call Amco Bank out by name until you're actually prepared to fight them. Alaska doesn't have that kind of power."

"We should put the flash drive somewhere safe," Rian said.

"Nothing could get into our vault," Fask said grimly.

"Tonight?" Carina asked plaintively. "It's been a very long day."

They all seemed to realize at the same time that it was getting quite late. The windows showed more reflection than anything, implying darkness beyond.

"Tomorrow is early enough," Fask said. "The van is safe within our gates. You should get some rest."

They all stood up from the table and each of them filed by Toren and Carina and shook their hands.

"Welcome to the madness," Raval told Carina with sympathy.

Tray took her into a full embrace, declaring, "I always wanted a sister!" Then he let go of her and added, "Besides Toren, I mean."

Toren almost hit him in the shoulder, but before he could, Carina had fixed Tray with an icy stare. "I presume that isn't some kind of sexist dig because you think a sister is somehow lesser than a brother."

Raval nearly fell over choking on his laughter and Tray, after a moment of surprise, gave a stumbling apology and looked entirely abashed.

Fask very gravely shook her hand. "I wish that we had had a chance to get to know each other under different circumstances, but know that you are very welcome in our family, and we all wish you every happiness."

See, that was kingly.

CHAPTER 25

Carina felt like everything was just a little surreal, like if she hadn't been wearing heavy hiking boots, she might have just floated away into space. Here she was, the honored guest of the royal family of Alaska, eating dinner with them while they planned her uncertain future.

"Can I see Shadow? Just to say goodnight?" she asked Toren as the last of the brothers shook her hand and gave her a formal welcome.

"Toren, if I could have a moment..." Fask said at the same time.

"I can show you the kennels, Carina," Tray volunteered.

Carina was loath to leave Toren's side, but she reminded herself that if they wanted to throw her to the proverbial wolves, they probably wouldn't string her along like this. She would be safe with Tray.

Toren kissed her goodbye, both of them embarrassed by the scrutiny of the others, and seemed as unwilling to let her go as she was to go.

Magic, Carina reminded herself.

Then she was walking with Tray down the stairs and out

the back. Tray, she recognized, was the ham of the family. She knew his type because she'd *been* his type, always looking for the joke.

"We only have one team left," Tray told her. "Dad used to race, but none of the rest of us took it up, and he let them age out and become housepets. A lot of people have adopted retired royal dogs."

"Dog racing?" Carina for a moment pictured greyhound racing and was confused.

"Dogsled racing," Tray explained. "We have enough to pull a sled, but I prefer to take out just one or two at a time and go skijoring. You can go almost as fast, but it's a lot freer. Just you, your dogs, and your skis."

The dog yard didn't look like much, just some boxes and loose straw over packed ground, scattered with gnawed rawhide and water dishes, but the tied up dogs were certainly happy and healthy looking. They all bounded to their feet when Tray and Carina appeared, barking and twisting around in delighted greeting.

"Mukluk, Anya, Jeebers, Angie, Thomas the Engine—he's our wheel dog." Tray introduced her to a dozen dogs, smaller than she had expected, all of whom wanted to lick her and lunge at the end of their runs and put their paws on her legs. "Dusty, Tanana, Sheba, Tricksy—she's slipped her collar more times than it should be possible. Dana, Shayla, and Phoebe. She's expecting a litter of puppies in a few weeks!"

Shadow was sulking on a lead near the back, but he rose to his feet at their approach and whined hopefully.

Carina sank down beside him in a pile of sweet, fresh straw, and buried her face in his ruff. Life had been so much simpler when it was just the two of them at her campsite. For the whole twenty minutes before Toren burst into her life and made it more complicated than *ever*.

Her chest ached.

She wanted to go back to being a nobody who knew *nothing*. Then she thought about *missing* meeting Toren, and the moment of loss was so sharp and deep that she was staggered.

She muttered nonsense into Shadow's fur about *good dogs* and *who's the best* until she was sure she wasn't going to cry in front of Tray, who, when she finally looked up, was abashedly trying to pretend like he wasn't feeling as awkward as she was.

"We can take you dog sledding once there's snow," he offered. "It's a lot different than snowmachining. No engine noise, just the swish of the sled and crunch of the snow. They go a lot faster than you might guess."

"Snow*machin*ing?" Carina was grateful for the neutral topic.

Tray smiled. "I think Americans call it snowmobiling."

"Oh, sure," Carina said, standing. Shadow pressed against her legs. "That would be fun." She gave him one last ruffle. "I'll give you a nice long walk tomorrow," she promised.

"It's really brave of you, what you've done," Tray said as she reluctantly drew away from Shadow.

"It's mostly stupid luck," Carina said. "And desperation."

CHAPTER 26

Watching Carina walk away from him with Tray was torture for Toren. Having to have *a talk* with Fask was worse.

"Let's sit," Fask suggested, leading Toren to the front of the second floor.

This was the big room, open to below, where they held diplomatic functions and seasonal parties. At one end was a low dais with chairs. They didn't look like thrones, exactly, being rather more plain and in the wood and iron motif of most of the castle, but they conveyed the power of the crown and were just enough higher than the rest of the room to look out over it.

There were seven chairs. Fask chose the throne to the right of their father's central perch and Toren could feel the choice he was being given: sit in the king's chair, or take the seat to Fask's right.

It was a test, and Toren had no idea what the right answer was. That was what his life was going to be from here on out, he realized with despair. One big series of tests.

Well, he wasn't king yet. Toren took the chair to Fask's right.

"You don't have to worry about anything," Fask told him warmly as they looked out over the empty room. The windows were like dark holes in the walls. "You know that I'll...that we'll have your back. We'll keep on keeping on just like we have, and we'll all make sure that you know what to say. It won't be so bad."

"It's going to be awful," Toren said. "No one wants me being the public face of anything."

Fask laughed, and Toren thought it sounded kind. "You're going to do fine," he assured Toren. "Just keep your chin up and step out strong."

Toren grinned crookedly. That had been Fask's advice when he was first starting to learn to skate. Step out strong. Timid steps inevitably meant falling.

"I'll try," he promised. Too bad this didn't come with hockey pads.

"And don't let Carina take all of the spotlight," Fask warned then.

Toren felt a shiver of defensiveness; he wasn't sure if it was his own feelings or his dragon's. "What do you mean?"

"She's strong-willed and smart," Fask said, sounding admiring. "The people will love her. But if you let her run away with all of the attention, it's going to look like a circus instead of a succession. Her story is exciting and dramatic. We need to downplay that as much as possible. I think you were right," he hastened to add. "It's best to come out in front of the information, take control of it instead of letting other parties twist it first. But this can't be all about her. This is about you. You becoming king. It has to be Alaska first, Carina second. People need to know where your priorities are."

Toren nodded slowly. That made sense.

"We should also fudge the timing a little. People might think a two-day romance is a little unreasonable."

"Happens in movies all the time," Toren said with a shrug. He disliked the idea of lying.

"Just...don't say how long you've known each other explicitly. You met while she was living in her van. There's no need to say that the spectacle at the hot springs was the very next day. The last thing we want to do is try to explain the real power of the Compact. Right now, people just believe we have peculiar traditions."

Secrets. So many secrets.

Toren was quiet, then nodded.

"Was it really love at first sight?" Fask asked curiously.

Toren remembered his first glimpse of Carina's hazel eyes. "It was more than that," he said with a sigh. "It was this...possibility. This brilliant certainty that I could be happier with this woman than I could ever imagine. It was knowing what she was, knowing how we could be...like I would never be complete without her. Like I never *had* been complete."

"How exactly did it happen?" Fask prodded. "Did you see her from the air and know?"

Toren considered. Had he known when he circled the clearing, when his dragon was weirdly focused on their task? Or even before that, when he had first gotten his assignment to encourage the squatter to move on? His dragon had insisted that they needed to go.

"I didn't really understand until I looked into her eyes," he explained thoughtfully. "But I felt a kind of pull before that. Like I was supposed to go there. Like I was supposed to go meet her."

Fask nodded thoughtfully. "Raval thought it might feel like a tug or a compulsion. He's suggested that a *potential* mate bond could be *activated,* without violating the Compact.

He's been investigating how to possibly awaken it, and use something like a dowsing rod."

"I can just see you, staggering around in the tundra with a forked stick," Toren teased. "Just to hit the ocean and realize she's on another continent."

Fask laughed with him. "Magic is generally impractical," he said agreeably. "But I'm going to have Raval continue on this track."

Toren felt a moment of hope. "Do you think one of you guys could find a mate? And I wouldn't have to be king?"

"We'll try," Fask promised. "But I don't know if we'll succeed. The Compact chooses, and it chose you, and usually, that's the end of it. You might as well get used to that chair." He hitched a shoulder towards the empty chair of their father.

"Kenth still thinks we should be trying to wake him up," Toren said thoughtfully. Kenth and Fask were oil and water, and Kenth spent most of his time outside of the capital city, avoiding inevitable conflict.

Grief passed over Fask's face. "I think we're beyond that," he said regretfully. "This can be how dragons pass, slow and silent. It's been so long...I think that father isn't really *in* there anymore."

"I never knew him very well," Toren said quietly. He had so many questions he wished he could ask.

"It's a pity," Fask said mournfully. "He taught me so many important things."

He shook himself, as if trying to shed grief off like a dog with a wet coat, and stood. "I'm going to call our lawyer, make sure he's here first thing tomorrow to start looking into the asylum angle. We'll protect Carina, Toren. Whatever it takes."

"War with America?" Toren didn't even want to think about it, rising to his feet beside Fask.

"I don't think it would come to that," Fask said firmly. "Let's hope it's all nothing more than a minor diplomatic strain." He stepped down off the dais.

Toren remained behind as his brother left, staring at the reflections in the dark windows, wondering what path his life was going to take from here. After a moment he turned and walked to his father's throne, sitting down into it gingerly.

It wasn't such a different view than he was used to, just a slightly different angle, a slightly larger chair.

And a huge responsibility.

CHAPTER 27

Tray walked Carina to the beginning of the third floor wing.

"I'm just down here, thanks," she said, hoping that her dismissal was the right combination of subtle and unmistakable. Her guards had fallen in a few paces behind them when they came in from the kennel, and they paused discreetly a little distance back.

"Have a good night," Tray said kindly. "And welcome to the family." He bowed over her hand and walked away merrily.

Carina was just wondering if she could somehow get rid of the guards as well, slowly walking down the hall to where she would pass Toren's door to get to her own, when she heard laughter and a wolf whistle around the corner where Tray had disappeared.

Toren, she thought in relief, just as she heard his voice saying, "Suck an egg, Tray!"

"Not very kingly, little brother," Tray teased him back.

Then Toren was stalking around the corner looking exasperated and her heart leaped in her chest.

The smile that bloomed on his scowling face when he saw her was so wonderful that Carina didn't even care if it was a magical compulsion, because she felt exactly the same, like the sun had just risen over her, or beautiful music had started playing somewhere.

"Carina," he said longingly, and they were both closing the distance between them and she was in his arms again at last.

"Oh, Toren," she said, feeling all undone and helpless and confused and *safe*.

For a moment, he just held her, and she sobbed into his shoulder as the day came crashing down around her. "I'm just an accountant," she cried. "I'm just a stupid person in the wrong place at the wrong time, with the wrong information. I can't possibly be a queen, I don't understand how all of this could happen, I'm so afraid..."

Tighter and tighter his arms got, and he was kissing her forehead and neck, and then he was picking her up and taking her into his rooms as if she weighed absolutely nothing.

His rooms were, if anything, larger than hers, but full of personal items, obviously not just guest quarters. He took her at once to his wide bed and laid her down and crawled in beside her and simply held her until the panic had ebbed away.

Faces close together, nose to nose, Carina took comfort from his breath, from his embrace, from the simple primal presence of him.

After a while, her sobs turned into whimpers and their touches turned from comfort to something more carnal.

She couldn't be close enough, couldn't feel enough of his skin under her fingers. Every touch was intense, every kiss was deep and desperate. She couldn't have said how they got out of their clothing, only knew that the feel of his skin was a panacea to all the ills of her life.

He was so strong, so sweet and kind, and when he filled her with his hard cock, Carina felt like the rest of the world simply went away, pleasure and gratification swelling inside of her like a musical phrase.

At first, they were side by side, slow and careful, but it grew more intense, and he rolled her onto her back, his weight protective and perfect as she fell from the heights of pleasure. He grew frantic, desperate, and Carina cried out in a second wave of bliss as he came deep inside of her and made noises of need and release.

They remained coupled long after they had finished, kissing and murmuring to each other. Carina wasn't sure what she said, or what he said, except that she was safe with him, and that...he loved her.

Afterwards, they washed together in a shower that could have fit five of them. They explored each other gently: the slopes of his shoulders, the small of his back, the framing of his hipbones. Her collarbones, the length of her neck, the place where ass became leg. He lifted her up against the cool tile wall of the shower and kissed her deeply as she wrapped her legs around him.

Everything felt perfect, when it was just the two of them, safe and private and bare, each to the other.

"I don't want to be king," he told her as they dried each other's backs.

She took a decadent second towel for just her hair, and replied sympathetically, "I don't want to be queen. I don't want to be a martyr. I don't want to be a crusader for justice."

"But here we are. King, queen, martyr, crusader." Toren took the towel from her and dried her hair more gently than she had been.

"It sounds like a book title."

"A terrible book they'd make you read in high school."

"And they'd want us to write a report on it exploring the underlying themes of *futility*."

"Speaking of futility," Toren said wryly, "I'm sorry for my family. They're a lot to take, and I think they embarrassed you."

Did he sometimes feel waves of emotion from her, the way she felt them from him? Carina wondered. Was that part of the spell? "They were fine," she assured him. "They had to ask the things they asked."

She could definitely feel the discomfort then, a confused, mixed-up hesitation. "And kids...?"

"Someday," she said thoughtfully. "I mean, I always figured I would, just not any time *soon*."

Relief, like a cool shower after a hot day, flowed from him. "Me, too."

"They're going to nag us ceaselessly, aren't they?" Carina said with dread...but not as much dread as she expected.

"It will definitely be a topic of discussion on my fan page," Toren groaned. "If it isn't already. Oh!" he said. "You're already internet famous."

Carina felt her stomach drop. "Hot topic on your fan page?"

"Front page of Yahoo and TMZ." Toren handed her his phone and Carina put a hand over her face. Sure enough, there she was, dripping wet in Toren's arms wearing her sister's plain bathing suit. There was another shot of her drinking water and looking wan while Toren gazed at her adoringly. The headline was: *Alaskan Prince Rescues Unknown Woman From Drowning At Angel Hot Springs*. A subtitle asked, *Wedding Bells for the Alaska Royal Family at Last?*

"I wasn't drowning," Carina protested feebly. "I was fainting."

"Tom-ay-toes, tom-ah-toes," Toren scoffed. He was

looking at her photo with the same besotted gaze he'd given her *in* the picture and Carina had a sudden stab of dismay that she hoped she stuffed down before it could escape her.

This mate thing really was like a magic spell. He clearly couldn't help himself, and there wasn't anything more to it than a random forced compulsion. It seemed like a poor way to pick a new queen, to Carina. Alaska itself couldn't possibly want her for their ruler, no matter how 'in name only' the title was.

Carina took the phone and scrolled through the articles, bemusedly reading speculation about who she was and shaking her head at some of the guesses. An island princess? Deposed Russian nobility? A European trust fund bunny? A server at the hot springs was quoted as saying she was some kind of sports celebrity.

Carina snorted.

It wouldn't be long before they uncovered her real identity.

Besides being American, and besides being wanted by the law because she'd stumbled across corruption in one of the largest banks in the world, who was she really? Nobody, that's who.

She was the most junior accountant in a big, completely anonymous financial firm. She didn't come from money. The closest she'd gotten to fame, before this, was a picture in the paper for winning a scholarship. There had been seven other people in the same photo. And none of them had been a prince.

It occurred to Carina that she was holding a phone. "Do you think I could call my sister?" she asked plaintively.

Toren hesitated. "We should check with Fask," he said cautiously. "Sorry."

Mrs. James, undoubtedly guessing that Carina would not be returning to her own room, had dropped off a pile of clothing for Carina that included a pair of pajamas and undergarments still in packaging that she gratefully wiggled into. Toren put on refreshingly pedestrian sweatpants and a t-shirt for a band called Gangly Moose.

It didn't feel like being royalty. It felt like sneaking into the honeymoon suite of a fancy hotel with a boy she'd just met. They curled up on his giant bed and talked about growing up and their favorite books and music. He liked old pulp novels like Doc Savage and modern action thrillers. She devoured historical romance. He liked an eclectic selection of bluegrass and jazz and rock, she had to giggle into a pillow as she admitted she liked pop music and boy bands.

"I'm not proud," she apologized as Toren made gagging noises.

"That's it," he said. "The wedding is off! Irreconcilable differences! It's doomed before it started!"

She had to tickle him for that, and they wrestled and kissed and finally slept, curled together under a thick down comforter, with moonlight spilling in through the open curtains.

CHAPTER 28

Toren woke blissfully, but even before his eyes were open, he remembered the week he was facing and his groan woke Carina.

"Sorry," he said, kissing her forehead.

"If I screw my eyes shut can I just keep sleeping and pretend that none of this is happening?" Carina asked plaintively.

"None of it?" Toren couldn't resist asking.

"Maybe some of it," Carina said, tipping her head to intercept his next kiss with her lips.

A knock on the door interrupted anything else that might have happened next and Carina gave a groan of her own.

"Your Highness," a loud voice called. "Breakfast is served."

Carina put her head under a pillow.

"Thank you," Toren called in return.

"We've got a helluva day ahead of us," Carina said, muffled.

"Let's get it started," Toren said with more confidence than he felt.

After a quick shower, Carina picked an outfit from the

pile of clothing that had been left for her and put her hair into a tidy, utilitarian braid. "I'll want to take Shadow for a walk after breakfast, if that's alright."

Toren started to say that they could ask Fask about the schedule, then remembered that he was going to have to make those kinds of decisions himself as king. "That sounds fine," he said. "Let's plan on eating lunch in Fairbanks. It's equinox, there's a festival downtown! I can show you around, and you can pick up anything you need in town."

"It sounds like my timing was good for once," Carina said wryly. "Do you have a spare toothbrush?"

"Under the sink!"

How had they fallen into such easy domesticity? Toren wondered. He liked to be alone, to have his space to himself whenever five brothers allowed such a thing. But now he couldn't imagine waking up without this woman, didn't want to picture his rooms without her.

Ours, his dragon reminded him, deeply satisfied. *As it should be. As it always will be.*

Breakfast was filled with dragging details about the engagement party, which Fask thought they should host the following weekend to coincide with the visiting royalty that had already been arranged. "That should give the most important people time to get here. I've got a press release written, and we can do questions with journalists later this morning."

He turned to Carina, who was nursing a cup of coffee and stabbing a sunny-side-up egg on her plate. "We'd like to get that flash drive into the vault as soon as possible for safe-keeping."

Carina cast a desperate look at Toren, who remembered that he'd promised to take her into town.

"After we do that, we were going to head in to Fairbanks to catch part of the festival," Toren said, as casually as he could manage. "We can do the press release later this afternoon." To his surprise, no one countered him, just accepted his amendment without question.

"I'll let you know where we'll do the press conference when I have the details," Fask agreed.

Carina gave a grateful smile to both of them and finished her coffee. The conversation centered around who would be invited to both the engagement party and the wedding itself.

"My sister?" Carina suggested tentatively, when they'd gotten down to second cousins and minor nobility from island nations.

"Certainly," Fask said. "Any family you wish. Give Mrs. James the details and she'll arrange the flights."

As the other brothers finished their meals and stood to go, Fask said across the table to Toren, "I want to talk to you about what you'll say to people."

"I was planning to go walk Shadow and assure him that I haven't abandoned him," Carina said. "Do you need me?"

Fask frowned. "I only want to caution you not to say too much yet. We'll coach you in specifics before the engagement party, but in the meantime, stick to 'it's classified,' and 'I can't say much.'"

Carina nodded solemnly. "I can do that." She gave Fask a wry smile. "I didn't get across two international borders by being gabby about my problems. I'm good at vague answers, don't worry."

Fask laughed. "I shouldn't underestimate you, my lady."

"Is it my lady now?" Toren wanted to know.

"Close enough," Fask said. "She'll officially be the fiancée of the crown prince of Alaska by next week, so let's get people used to it. *Your Highness* won't be appropriate until you are married, and *Your Majesty* will be after the coronation, of course."

Toren filed the information and Carina gave him a brief

kiss on the cheek before heading out to walk Shadow. Two of the guards at the door peeled away to follow her at a slight distance.

"Is she in *danger?*" Toren asked Fask quietly after she'd left.

"We'll have guards trailing her any time she isn't with one of us," Fask said confidently. "I've already got the local police quietly on alert; there will be extra patrols downtown at the festival as well."

Toren wasn't sure that really answered the question, but it did make him feel better.

"Make sure your phone is on," Fask reminded him. "And no ignoring it."

Toren grinned. He was notorious for not answering messages.

He glanced back as he heard swift footsteps at the door, and was stepping to meet Carina almost before he registered the expression on her face. "What's wrong?" he asked.

"Shadow," Carina said miserably. "He's gone."

Behind her, Tray was holding Shadow's blue and gold collar in his hands and looking almost as distressed as she was.

"He slipped his collar sometime last night. I went out to feed them this morning and he was gone."

Toren folded Carina into a comforting embrace, but she remained stiff and distant, inconsolable in the loss he could sense from her. "That's twice now that I've lost him, you'd think I'd be used to this by now," she sniffed.

"I checked the fit of his collar yesterday," Tray protested, looking guilty. "It was properly sized. I don't know how it happened."

"He's a bit of an escape artist," Toren said to his brother. Then, to Carina, "We can check at the animal shelter while we're downtown, maybe put up fliers."

Carina wiped her face on her sleeves, clearly trying to regain her composure. Toren was keenly aware of Fask watching them and he was irritated that they were always going to be under that kind of scrutiny. "Maybe he's just off exploring and he'll come back for supper," he said optimistically, guiding Carina away. "Let's go check around the garage and get the flash drive."

CHAPTER 29

Toren's concept of a garage was much different than Carina's. It was more like a giant *Batcave*, and was *full* of cars. There were vintage cars, muscle cars, race cars, two limos, a Jeep, several pick-up trucks, and a handful of motorcycles. There were a few four-wheelers and several snowmobiles. No, wait, Tray had called them snow*machines*. It was a hodgepodge of styles and tastes, well-lit, and much cleaner than Carina expected from a garage; it still had that tangy smell of oil and metal, but the concrete was spotless and the workbenches were tidy.

Her sister's van looked terribly out of place near the end where they came in, with its dents and rust. It looked as though they had washed it, but nothing short of an overhaul and a paint job would make it fit in with the royal fleet.

Kind of like Carina herself, she thought miserably.

Shadow was nowhere to be found, though she'd yelled herself hoarse in a circuit around the large building. Maybe he didn't recognize his name, she thought. After all, she'd just assigned it to him randomly two nights before. She had no claim over him. Not even the kind of tenuous magical claim that she had on Toren.

Raval was there, tinkering with one of cars. He nodded at Toren and Carina as they came in, and even asked, "Did you find the dog?"

Carina shook her head, not trusting herself to talk, and Toren squeezed her hand. "We'll keep looking," he said to both of them. "He's come back before."

Carina squeezed him back, wishing he felt hopeful, and they walked around the far side of the van...where they drew to a halt.

There was broken glass on the cement.

In this immaculate garage, there were fragments of broken glass scattered on the clean, white cement.

Broken headlight glass.

Toren figured out what it meant before Carina could put the pieces together in her head.

"Raval, has anyone been in here this morning? Call the guards! I want security here immediately. Maybe the police... we need to look for evidence. We need photos. Get Fask! Oh, I'll call him."

His voice was just nonsense in Carina's head as she walked forward, her hiking boots crunching over the shards.

The headlight was completely broken out, and when she reached her hand into the cavity, she knew what she would find.

"It's gone," she whispered. "It's *gone*."

The only proof that she had of the crime she'd found, the only evidence that would carry any weight in the fight for justice and her own freedom...it had been stolen.

"Who knew?" Toren asked her. "Who knew where the drive was?"

The rest of the van was untouched. It was a surgical

THE DRAGON PRINCE OF ALASKA

extraction, someone had known exactly where it had been hidden.

"No one," Carina said, hearing the note of hysteria in her voice. "We never told your brothers or the captain where in the van it was, only that it was there. You and I were the only ones who knew where I hid it."

Toren frowned. "Your sister?"

"I didn't tell her," Carina said, choking down her fear. "I figured out the hiding place myself, right before the Canadian border. I felt pretty clever for it, too." She tried to laugh and failed.

"Could someone have seen you at the hot springs when you showed me where it was?" Toren said, brows furrowed. "Maybe someone was watching with binoculars? There was that man in the restaurant who kept staring at us, and we know that *someone* tracked you *to* the resort."

Carina shrugged one shoulder, feeling like her whole body was somehow numb and on fire at the same time. This wasn't at all how things were supposed to be going.

The garage door opened and the whole place felt suddenly smaller as a dozen guards swarmed in with a blast of cold air and began taking photos and asking questions and poking around in the small space between the van and the next vehicle.

The captain frowned fiercely at Carina as if it was her fault personally, and then crisply sent several people to check the perimeter and draw up logs and camera footage. Fask quizzed Raval, who hadn't seen anyone since he'd come in after breakfast.

"It must have happened last night," Fask said, frowning. "Are you alright, Carina?"

Carina could only stare at him. No, she wasn't alright. She was a fugitive. The last tenuous hope for clearing her name had just been *stolen*. She felt like she'd been punched in the gut and was gasping for air.

She felt *delirious*.

"What can I do?" Toren asked Fask. "How can I help?"

"You can't," Fask said dismissively.

"Does this change our plans?" Toren asked, and for a moment Carina thought he was talking to her.

"No," Fask said. "But we're sending guards with you into town."

"Do you still want to go?"

That was for her, this time, and Carina turned away from the people sweeping up the glass and nodded numbly. "Sure." Pretend it was normal. Pretend any of this was normal.

The security footage outside the garage showed Shadow, to Carina's grief. There wasn't a camera on the dog yard, or inside the garage, but he loped into the frame for a few moments, sniffing around the building, then vanished. Shortly after, the cameras had gone down, presumably when the person after the flash drive broke in.

"The wires were cut. Someone knew exactly where to clip them." The captain was furious, and everyone else ranged from agitated to angry.

Carina was glad when she could finally escape with Toren in a car with Grim and Amused, who looked far less amused than he had when she had named him in her head.

"Carina..."

"I can't," she said fiercely, voice low. "It's too raw to talk about it all now, and I'm not going to. We're going to a festival and I'm going to forget about all of it for a little while and we're going to figure it all out later, okay?"

Comfort. He felt like comfort and safety, even now, when Carina was starting not to believe in either of those things.

"I'm here whenever you're ready," he told her. "Let's have a fun time, eat some food, pretend we're not involved in breaking up big corporate cons, not royalty, not missing Shadow. No, wait, we'll stop at the shelter first and file a report. Then we'll pretend we're not any of those things for a few hours and I'll show you a little of the city."

"I'd like that," Carina said, and she thought, with Toren at her side, that she could actually enjoy it.

CHAPTER 30

Shadow wasn't at the animal shelter, and none of the missing dog posters matched his description. Toren left his details and the woman at the counter solemnly promised to call if the dog was turned in.

Carina seemed to take it well. Toren could feel the stress, leaking out around her like a poorly sealed beach ball, but she *trusted* him, trusted that he—that his family—could protect her.

He would do anything not to betray that trust, he thought, giving her a sidelong look as they climbed from the car.

She looked absolutely determined to enjoy herself, as if she could will herself into happiness.

Downtown Fairbanks was decked out for autumn equinox, with Alaska flags flying from every building. The bridge across the Chena River had been decorated in fall garlands, and there was a brass band playing at the memorial park by the river. Open booths were set up lining First and Second Avenue, both closed to motorized traffic. They were filled with vendors selling crafts and furs and food.

They heard the festival, then smelled it, and then rounded the corner into happy chaos. A dance troupe was keeping warm with a stomping Russian dance, the audience cheering happily as they squatted and flung their feet out in classic form. A trio of spangled belly dancers were waiting at the side of the stage, huddled in coats as they anticipated their turn.

"I'm starving," Carina said, nose in the air. Breakfast had been hours ago.

"Got a preference?" Toren asked. There was an international selection: American pizza, Thai food, Greek pitas and gyros, sandwiches of many varieties, hot dogs, and more.

"What's Alaskan?" Carina asked. "Pretend I'm a tourist. I mean, I basically *am*."

"Ah," Toren said knowingly. "I know just the booth."

He led her down the street and around the corner as the bellydancers gave a loud *zhagaroot* to announce the start of their routine.

A busy booth boasted caribou sausages in buns and salmon burgers, with chips and local-made pickles.

Carina, after agonizing a few moments, chose a salmon burger, and they went to the riverside park to sit and eat.

Carina was shivering. "I'm going to have to find a second hand store and buy a warmer coat," she said. Although it was sunny and the sky was brilliant blue, it wasn't terribly warm; there was a biting breeze that promised the coming winter. "How are my clothes going to work out?" she asked. "I was half-expecting ball gowns to be laid out on my bed in the morning, and I don't know how queenly my hiking boots are."

"It doesn't matter how you dress most of the time," Toren assured her. "There are some formal affairs, but even at those, you'll find that one guy in overalls stained with chainsaw oil. Tray practically lives in hockey jerseys. It's Alaska; we're practical and independent, and we rarely dress to impress each other."

"How refreshing," Carina said, taking the last bite of her food.

"Admit it," he teased her. "You were hoping for the frilly dresses and tiaras."

To his delight, Carina laughed. "Well, come on, if I'm going to be a princess, I want to do it *right*." She considered, then added, "I have to admit, I'm *glad* I don't have to wear heels."

Toren wiped his hands on napkins and stood. A couple of girls sitting nearby were eyeing them curiously, whispering together. "It's not him," one of them said clearly.

"I have an idea," he said. "She's usually down this way." He took Carina's hand decisively and they went down First Avenue to the end. They didn't make very fast progress; the booths along their way were filled with arts and crafts and Carina dawdled, admiring the carvings and dolls and masks. She didn't offer to buy anything, but she did compliment the vendors, who smiled at her and grinned at Toren. He recognized a good number of them from previous festivals and was *sure* they recognized him.

The crowd swirled around them, cheerful and full of celebration. Children went bolting around them, some of them with dogs on leashes.

When they arrived at the crafters at the end of the aisle, Carina's mouth made a very satisfying O.

"Pick something out," Toren said. "Hi, Anna."

A large, smiling Native Alaskan woman was sitting in a booth filled with parkas and hats and mittens, all in luxurious fur and colorful fabric patterns. She was beading on a pair of fur slippers, a wild rose pattern in bright pink.

"Toren, you scamp. If you knock over a display, you're paying for the whole thing."

"I haven't knocked over one of your racks since I was eleven," Toren protested, bending close to kiss her on the cheek. "I'm a little less clumsy than I was then, and you are no less lovely."

"No less of a suck-up than you ever were, either," Anna scolded him. She looked appraisingly at Carina. "You're with this one, then?"

Carina scrambled forward in the narrow space and offered her hand. "Hi," she said shyly, ducking around the coats. "I'm Carina."

Anna's handshake was firm and calloused. "Nice to meet you," she said briefly. "Can I help you find something?"

"Oh no," Carina said quickly, though she shivered. "I don't have this kind of money…"

"It's my treat," Toren said swiftly. "Don't worry."

Carina gave him a hesitant glance.

"He owes me a sale, for all the ones he's lost me over the years," Anna said shrewdly. "Always running through with his rowdy brothers like he owns the place, putting dirty fingerprints on the wares, scaring the customers. Pull down that teal parka, Toren, see how it suits her."

"We *do* own the place, Anna," Toren teased her. He picked out a pull-over parka in a flowered teal-green pattern that matched her hazel eyes, trimmed in mink.

Anna snorted. "You own the *land*. You *earn* the people. Now hold that up for her. Yes, try it on."

Carina took off her light jacket and wriggled into it, pulling the generous hood up over her head to test the fit. "I would never in a million years get cold in this," she said in wonder. Toren wisely decided not to mention that this was only a medium-weight parka, and she'd need something warmer to be out in the bitterest cold of winter.

The crafter laughed and pulled out a full-length mirror. Carina twisted to see the back. It covered her sweet ass, which Toren thought was a shame but he accepted the concession as important to warmth.

"That's mink on the hood," Anna pointed out. "My son traps them out on the flats. Won't frost when you're out in the cold."

There was beautiful embroidery tape all along the cuffs and hem, twining forget-me-nots and wild roses. Toren unwound the price tag from one of the buttons before Carina could see it. "We'll take it," he told Anna.

"I should think so," Anna snorted. She took the credit card Toren offered. "You need a bag?"

"Can I wear it?" Carina asked wistfully.

Anna looked pleased. "If you have any problems with it, you come see me. All of my work is guaranteed for craftsmanship."

"It's so beautiful," Carina told her, eyes gleaming suspiciously as she hugged herself. "Thank you so much."

Anna waved them off. "You're blocking the way for other paying customers," she scolded them.

"This is an amazing festival for a town this size," Carina said, as they continued to wander among the booths and enjoy the entertainment; there was a woman juggling knives and a man in drag doing fortunes.

"This is one of our smaller ones," Toren said offhandedly, though he was pleased by Carina's happiness. "The summer solstice festival is our biggest event—it goes two blocks further and runs until midnight."

"With fireworks?" Carina teased.

"No fireworks," Toren said. "You can't see them in the summer because it doesn't get dark. We save those for New Year's."

Carina blinked. "I hadn't thought of that." She laughed.

"The queen of Alaska ought to know that," she said sheepishly, shaking her head. Then, "Do you know everyone?"

Toren, caught in the act of waving at one of the other vendors, chuckled. "Not everyone," he protested. "But the city isn't that big, and you see a lot of familiar faces at these things. We...used to make more regular appearances at festivals when I was younger, but we don't do it so much now."

"Now that your dad is...sick. Sleeping."

"He loved this kind of thing, walking among the crowds, being one of them, listening to their problems firsthand," Toren said thoughtfully. "He never acted like being a king made him better than anyone else." He heard the longing in his voice before he recognized it in his chest. People had stopped asking about his father, he'd been absent so long. The gregarious man he remembered had been replaced by an impression of isolation.

They paused to listen to a bluegrass band. "They aren't *bad*," Carina conceded. A loose dog bolted around them, chased by a swearing owner, and Toren watched sorrow wash over her face.

"Do you think Shadow came back to the castle?" she asked wistfully.

At that moment, the phone in Toren's pocket buzzed. Hope swirled between them as he pulled it out. "Fask wants us back at the palace for the press release," he said, disappointed, but not nearly as disappointed as Carina was. "Was there anything else you wanted to see?"

Carina shook her head. "No, I'm ready to go back."

"They're going to love you," Toren promised. Then, hesitantly, "Will you quiz me on my speech on the way back? Fask sent notes for both of us."

"I'd love to," Carina said. "I was in a high school production of My Fair Lady, so I know all about *e-nun-ci-A-tion*."

He took her hand and nodded back at the guards who were trailing them discreetly.

Just for just a moment, the crowd parted and he saw the same man he'd seen at Angel Hot Springs, standing with his arms crossed, avidly watching Carina.

Then a group of laughing tourists walked between them, and when Toren tried to spot the man again, he was gone, lost in the crowd.

CHAPTER 31

The drive to the palace was as beautiful as their first trip was, but Carina watched very little of it. Their practice of the speech was very silly, Toren trying at first to very solemnly read his cards, but swiftly descending into a mockingly officious voice. "We have gathered," he said, twirling an imaginary mustache, "to make an announcement of the gravest urgency," he improvised.

Then he switched to a panicked voice. "You guys have to help me! They're making me get married! Tell the press! Get me out of here! It's a traaaaap! Oh, noooooo!"

Carina mimed a frying pan, and they collapsed together in the seat of the car, laughing and glancing forward at Grim and Amused in the front seats. The two guards were trying very hard to keep straight faces.

She was still smiling, even when they arrived at the castle and found the press set up on the front steps. She was with Toren, and she was *safe* with Toren.

"I suppose we have to do this," Carina said, as the car pulled up into the drive and she got a glimpse of the press vehicles crowding the circle. "No going back."

They both sighed at the same time, and then the guards were opening the door to the car and helping Carina out.

Cameras turned to them as they came walking down the sweeping sidewalk to the castle, hand in hand, and they were greeted with a chaos of questions. Fask had set up a podium on the steps, and Toren drew Carina close as the microphone crackled and the noise died down.

Toren was quiet, staring out at them, for so long that Carina wondered if he'd gotten stage fright. She clung tight to his hand and tried to project every scrap of confidence she could at him.

He turned to her as if he'd felt it, and gave her a slow smile so sexy and adoring that Carina couldn't help but grin back at him.

"Thanks for being here," he said, finding the correct distance from the microphone after a false start. That was not at all how Fask's speech had started. "I'm really delighted to introduce you to Carina Andresen, and announce that she's agreed to marry me. I understand that you've probably heard a lot of crazy stuff and we can't really answer questions about that right now, so please don't be jerks about it, but if you want to know about how great she is or how happy we are, I have plenty to say about that."

Everyone laughed, like they were supposed to, and no one wanted to look like a jerk on record after that, so the questions were all very simple and Toren answered what he could while Carina smiled and blushed and waved. At the very end, she leaned forward to the microphone and said "Thank you," and everyone applauded.

"That wasn't as bad as I'd feared," she said with a sigh of relief as they walked up the steps to the castle and the press started to disband behind them.

"You got creative with the speech," Fask said with a

frown, meeting them halfway up the stairs, but he didn't really seem bothered.

"Your speech was boring," Toren said merrily. "And I didn't say anything I shouldn't have."

"You did fine," Fask said grudgingly.

They were almost to the great doors when the big glass panel very suddenly shattered before her eyes and Toren was diving on top of her, driving her to the ground. She heard stitches rip.

"There's a shooter!" someone cried. "Get down!"

"Where is it coming from?"

"What's going on?"

"It must have come from over there..."

"Tell me you got that on tape!"

Beneath Toren's arm, Carina had a glimpse of Fask, snarling and shouting.

"Inside, Your Highnesses," Captain Luke said, very close by, and then Carina and Toren were being hauled up and hurried inside. She had just enough time to see a shadow in the air, and a vague ripple of light. None of the press members seemed to notice it, but Carina suspected one of the brothers had taken off to try to hunt down the shooter.

The *shooter*.

Someone had *shot* at her.

Carina felt like she was boiling inside.

Someone had stolen her evidence and tried to shoot her and her new parka had probably been torn in the fall, and her dog was lost, and she felt like a feral cat trapped in a corner. She might go down, but she was going to take someone's face off when she went.

Then they were inside, being rushed to the back of the lobby, while Captain Luke muttered furiously about the defensibility of giant glass panels in doors and the idiocy of architects.

"How'd the press release go?"

Tray, oblivious to the drama, was coming from the back entrance, but Carina wasn't looking at him whatsoever; all of her attention was on the shape beside him.

"Shadow!" She shook off Toren's hand and bolted across the hall to slide on her knees the last few steps as the big dog capered to meet her, tongue happily lolling from the side of his mouth. His tail was wagging furiously, and he wriggled and tried to lick Carina as she threw her arms around him.

Gray fur flew everywhere as she wrestled and scratched him, and he fell on his side in happiness.

"Where did you find him?" Carina asked, looking up at Tray as she wiped tears from her eyes.

Tray, looking pleased and relieved, shrugged. "He just came back," he said helplessly. "He showed up just a few moments ago looking hungry and tired. He's got a bit of a limp, careful with that front leg. He probably had a grand time *somewhere*. What's going on? What happened to the door?"

"We just got shot at!" Toren said, outraged, hovering just behind Carina.

"What?!"

"I didn't hear a shot," Carina said, still confused and feeling shocky with relief. She had Shadow back.

"It was too far away," Fask snapped. "The shooter might have been a half a mile away with good optics. You'd only hear the impact, not the explosion."

Carina thought he sounded more irritated than scared. Here she was, being more of a problem than *ever*.

CHAPTER 32

Toren reminded himself that he didn't need to be jealous of a dog. Carina's joy at Shadow's return was strong and pure and washed away all of the terror of being shot at; if it weren't for the tense swirl of the guards and the missing glass panel in the door, he might have thought he'd imagined the assassination attempt.

Then he remembered that *someone had shot at Carina*, and he felt rage blaze through his veins until he wasn't sure how much of it was his and how much of it was his simmering dragon's. Possibly, some of it was Carina's.

He gave Shadow a suspicious look, but if the dog was a shifter, he was a master method actor, acting in every way like a common dog. Besides, Tray already had him in hand when the shooting had occurred. Which reminded Toren again that *someone had shot at Carina.*

Fask was quietly talking to Captain Luke, and Toren left Carina's side to uncharacteristically insert himself into their private conversation. "I want to know what we're doing to increase security," he said quietly, as firmly as he could.

Fask and Luke both looked at him in surprise.

"Luke and I can handle this," Fask told him. "You worry about—"

"About how I'm keeping my *mate* safe?" Toren suggested. "Because that's a big part of what I intend to worry about."

"You don't need to know the details," Fask said impatiently. "It would take too much time to bring you up to speed. You don't understand how anything here is run."

Toren felt stung. "Well, maybe I should."

Fask and Luke stared at him. Fask looked irritated, but Luke had an approving smile on her usually inscrutable face.

"I'm going to be the king of Alaska," Toren reminded them both. "I *should* know how everything is run. I should be part of...refining our defenses...or...whatever."

Fask gentled. "You don't need to know all the gritty details to be king," he said.

"You do," Toren pointed out. "You know how everything works, and everyone agrees that makes you the best candidate for the job. So how come when I want to learn all of that, you just brush me off? I don't want to just be a king, I want to be a *good* king." They both looked at him with deeply complicated expressions and Toren scrambled to add, "I mean, I don't *want* to be king...but if I'm going to be..."

Fask frowned thoughtfully. "Alright—"

Raval returned then, in a blaze of light, and shifted back to human on the front steps. The press had been herded away to write their shocking headlines and the castle staff had already taped clear plastic over the door and swept up the glass.

"I found the gun and the place the shooter must have been," Raval reported, handing over the weapon and an empty cartridge. "But they were already gone. It's a bluff with no foot access, nearly impossible for human access. It was a shifter, at least, almost certainly something that can fly, if I couldn't find them."

Fask gave a hiss of dismay and Luke actually growled.

"Does Amco Bank hire *shifters?*" Toren blurted, still thinking about Shadow.

"This isn't Amco Bank's work," Fask snarled.

Toren looked at him blankly, then the rest of the pieces fell into place. "One of our enemies under the Compact?"

"If you...or Carina...come to an unfortunate end before the Compact is renewed, Alaska is out, and open for takeover."

The idea that the shooter might have been shooting at him was almost a relief. It meant Carina was that tiniest bit safer.

But of course, it was the same outcome, no matter which of them was eliminated, until the actual coronation, so they were both still in terrible danger.

Something occurred to him. "Someone was watching Carina," he said. "Or maybe both of us. At the hot springs, and again at the festival."

He had everyone's attention. "It was a big man, taller than me, dark hair, olive skin."

Luke took as detailed a description as Toren could give, which wasn't very, and he was frustrated by his inability to be more helpful as the discussion turned to the involvement of the police to spread out their efforts to find the culprit.

He looked over to find Carina still sitting on the floor with Shadow, arms wrapped around him as his tail beat out an irregular rhythm on the warm wooden planks. Guards were around her in a loose semi-circle. She looked very small and lost.

"Go on," Fask said quietly to him, as Luke quizzed Raval for more details about the site of the assassination attempt.

Toren startled, looking at him. "I was serious about doing more, about learning everything. I don't want to be a paper king."

"It can wait," Fask said sympathetically. "You can't do everything at once, and your mate needs you right now."

Fask didn't have to tell him twice. He barely had to say it once. Everything in Toren yearned to be with Carina, to hold her in his arms and shield her from harm. Knowing how close she'd come to being shot...If he lost her...

The guards melted back as he knelt next to Carina and gathered both her and Shadow in for an embrace.

"Oh, Toren," she said, leaning her head against him. "I'm tired of being a *target*."

"If it makes you feel any better, they might have been shooting at *me*."

"That doesn't make me feel the slightest bit better," Carina said, but she laughed and squeezed Toren back.

"Come on, let's go get Shadow set up with a water dish and a rug in our room."

Carina dragged a hand over her face, dashing away tears that she seemed surprised to find there. "Won't Mrs. James have objections to that?" she asked with a hiccup as she rose to her feet with Toren. Shadow stood and leaned against her knees.

"Let her," Toren said boldly. "I'm going to be the king of Alaska. It's got to come with *some* perks."

CHAPTER 33

"You said you'd be keeping a low profile!" June said furiously when Carina finally got her to pick up her phone. "And instead, you're all over the covers of the checkout stand magazines. In *my swimsuit*. That is not a low profile, Carina. That is the opposite of a low profile!"

Carina could hear the tears in her sister's voice. "Nothing has gone exactly like I planned," she confessed. "I'm sorry I couldn't call sooner."

"I know you probably couldn't," June sobbed. "But oh, wow, Carina, I've been so worried. They've been asking and asking and asking...and there are people constantly watching..."

Carina was crying now, too. "I'm so sorry. I never wanted to drag you into this."

"You're a princess!" June yelled. "I want to be dragged into that part!"

"I'm not a princess yet," Carina laughed tearfully. "But I want you to come up here for that. For a while. To be...safe."

"Is...there danger? Do they still think...?"

"We probably shouldn't talk much about it over the phone," Carina said reluctantly. "But John can come. They'll cover everything, travel, places to stay here, jobs, even."

"My job can kiss my ass," June agreed, sobbing again. "Cari, I'm so happy for you and so scared!"

They talked for a while about trivial things: the weather in Alaska, Carina's travels. They didn't mention the shooting. "You'd better not have put a single scratch on my van," June threatened.

Carina thought about the slashed seats and the broken headlight. "It's *pristine*," she lied, knowing that her sister would hear the fib. They laughed hysterically. "I'll pay you back," Carina promised. "I love you, Juney."

"I love you, too, Princess Cari," June wept.

Carina washed her face and cuddled with Shadow, who didn't particularly want to be cuddled, then went to find Toren.

He was in the so-called informal dining room with Rian, who nodded and invited her in.

"There was a case in Finland where they held a ninety-six day religious ceremony for a refugee while they negotiated with her government, so I've got a few ideas for things we can do with you if things get touchy about extradition," he said reassuringly.

"That's a relief," Carina said. Shadow lay down on the floor at her feet as she sat next to Toren and she let his leash rest on the arm of her chair. Even in the castle, she was making a practice of keeping him leashed, because he'd demonstrated a habit of bolting, and because she wanted to give Mrs. James as little grief as possible.

"I've also been in touch with the woman who was writing that thesis on the unaltered copy of the Compact," Rian continued. Carina noticed that color rose in his cheeks. "We've had some really interesting exchanges, and she has some theories I'm going to be looking into more carefully about mates. We might be able to *make* one happen for Fask. It's...kind of an awkward conversation at times because she doesn't know what mates are, and she thinks the dragon and magic references are code for something. I...might need to go see her in person."

Toren gave Rian a distinctly skeptical look. "You hate traveling."

"I could fly," Rian said.

"You could fly to Florida and talk to some stranger about a Compact she probably thinks she imagined," Toren proposed sarcastically.

Rian nodded in full seriousness. "It's not really fair to her. I mean, we basically destroyed her thesis by replacing the Compact. She probably thought she was going crazy."

"You've got to be careful about what you tell her," Toren cautioned. Then he smiled and laughed. "Have *I* ever said 'be careful' to *you*? Isn't this supposed to be the other way around?"

Rian grinned back at him. "Yeah, well, things are changing, Your Crown Highness."

"Never call me that again," Toren groaned.

When Toren rose to go, Rian stopped him. "Toren, when you first felt the mate bond...it was *before* you met Carina, wasn't it?"

Toren stopped and Carina watched his face curiously, aching a little. She was already standing, and Shadow was swirling at her feet, bored and restless.

"Yes," he said slowly, staring into space. "It was when you first told me what my job was, to evict the squatter. I mean, that's usually the last thing in the world I would want to do, and I was already trying to find an excuse to get out of it. But my dragon insisted that we needed to go, that it was really important, and I knew he was *right*. And that only got stronger, the closer we got."

He seemed to jolt back into himself, and the look he gave Rian was shrewd. "Why do you ask?"

Carina was sure she saw Rian blush then.

"Nothing," Rian said swiftly. "No reason."

A terrible thought occurred to Carina as they parted ways.

If one of the other brothers found their mates, they wouldn't have any reason to protect her. They'd made it clear that Toren was the least likely and least desirable brother to make king. And if they didn't need her to ensure that he *became* king...

She was nothing but trouble to them, a political problem of epic proportions. An embarrassment. A complication.

If another brother found a nice mate with half as much baggage, they'd have no reason to fight her extradition. And without any evidence...

"Are you alright?" Toren asked, and Carina gave him a wan smile. She couldn't seem to feel what he was feeling—maybe because her own emotions were feeling so raw—but she could see the concern in his eyes and she'd learned to read his face. She hesitated a moment, wanting to tell him all of her doubts about *them*, and share the confusion she had about all of her feelings and fears. But he was already carrying arguably more load on his shoulders than she was, and he seemed blissfully content to believe that their love was magically undeniable and unshakable. She didn't want to take even a moment of that happiness from him.

"I'm fine," Carina said. "Just...it's all a lot sometimes."

Toren put his arm around her shoulders warmly. "Believe me, I know. Fask and Mrs. James have us booked non-stop for the next few days. You've got deportment lessons, and dancing instructors, and I get to learn how to apply royal seals, and there are going to be hours with the lawyers, and it's all going to be just fine, because we've got each other, and we'll get through this."

Shadow gave a canine cough like he was going to throw up.

"For now," Toren proposed, "let's take Shadow for a walk and I'll show you the pond and the ridge trail and we'll pretend we're going to run away."

CHAPTER 34

The days to the engagement party passed like runaway trains, sweeping Toren along while he hung on for dear life and tried to pack as much into his head as he possibly could.

"You want a book on...what?"

Rian's surprise was understandable as he put the lid to his laptop down.

Toren moved into Rian's library, eyeing the shelf-lined walls speculatively. "Tax structures and capital expenses. Did you know that it cost more than five million Alaskan dollars to repair the North Haul Road after that big flood two years ago? I had no idea how much *dirt* costs."

"You know, Toren, you don't have to learn *everything* in order to be king," Rian reminded him. "You'll *have* advisors."

"I want to know when my advisors are full of crap," Toren said flatly. "Already this week, I've had people coming after me with...the craziest stuff. People clearly sucking up, people with all these genuine-looking problems and complaints, people who want favors, people who want to yell at me for screwing things up when I'm not even technically engaged yet, let alone making decisions."

"Isn't that all supposed to go through the press secretary?" Rian said. "Doesn't he screen everything?"

"I told him I wanted to see it all," Toren sighed. "That might have been a mistake. Oh, I also want to look at the Compact."

"I'll get something on the taxes," Rian said. "And you can chat with the PS about throttling back on what he sends through. But why do you want to see the Compact?"

"It's a big part of why we're doing everything we're doing, and I want to understand it."

Rian laughed dryly. "No one understands the Compact!" he scoffed. "It took all of the Small Kingdoms casters and a five-hundred year old dragon to make it, and no one is alive who wrote it, and it is seven hundred pages of complex spell that is supposed to save the world. Better men than you have tried to make sense of it. No offense."

Toren wasn't offended. "I'd still like to look at it," he said. "I should do that much before I'm bound by it. Especially if I'm going to sign the Renewal. I don't think that should be the first time I tried to read it."

Rian smiled at him kindly. "You've been working really hard this week," he observed. "Everyone is impressed."

"I don't want to let anyone down," Toren confessed. "I didn't ask for this, and I don't want it, but I want to do it right if I'm going to."

"Well, you're not going to do it right if you have a mental breakdown," Rian advised. "Why don't you take the rest of the day off. We can check out the Compact in the vault after your big engagement party this weekend. Go take Shadow for a walk with Carina, play some video hockey or whatever you usually do. You can't do for everyone else before you do for you."

"Dad used to say that," Toren remembered abruptly.

"He wasn't wrong," Rian insisted. "Go spend some of your last free time with your mate."

Toren sighed, but he knew that Rian was right.

He found Carina in her van, still parked in the garage. The sliding door was open and Shadow was on a leash sulking at her feet. The big gray dog had been caught trying to escape twice, and seemed to resent being kept under close surveillance.

Carina herself was sitting on the back bench, a well-folded brochure about Alaska in her hands. Toren recognized it; he hated that one because it had a photo of himself as a kid, and he remembered how agonizing posing for that picture had been. Kenth and Fask had been arguing. Tray had been teasing Rian. Their father had been more patient than Toren thought they deserved.

Toren sat down beside her and she leaned into him as he put an arm around her shoulders. As always, he felt that bubble of peace and rightness that he always felt with her. Was it hers? His dragon's? He seemed to feel her emotions less than he had at first.

It is right, his dragon murmured. *It was meant to be.*

No matter how crazy things got, no matter how full with information his head felt, or how full of frustration he was with *how things actually worked* versus *how things ought to work*, every time that he found Carina and held her, everything was *better*.

This was what having a mate could be, he thought with contentment. For all of the weight and duty that had come with finding her, he couldn't once regret it.

She tipped her head up and kissed him, twining her fingers into his, and he could feel her relaxing, all through her body.

"Planning our big escape?" Toren asked. "Are we going to

drive to Mexico? Do you have something picked out in South America?"

"I haven't quite worked out passports," Carina chuckled. She still hadn't been issued identification, and the United States hadn't officially pressed for extradition or acknowledged that they would. She was in a terrible, stressful limbo, and Toren was awed by how well she had held up under the strain.

Some nights, she confessed her fears and cried in his arms, and Toren told her all the ways he dreaded failing, and they comforted each other in every way that they could.

But publicly, she showed a brave face, smiling and laughing and picking her way through all of the new complications and dangers that had been thrust at her with her chin high and her eyes dancing. She was funny and kind, and Alaska already loved her. She was a better princess than any of them had any reason to expect, and she would be a better queen than they deserved, Toren thought.

"Hey, you want to play a round of hockey?" he asked abruptly.

"I know it's cold, but it hasn't been *that* cold," Carina chuckled. "And I can't skate anyway..."

"We can play field hockey," Toren said, tugging at her arm with enthusiasm. "Come on, I'll show you."

Shadow, suspecting excitement, surged to his feet and tried to bolt.

Carina grabbed his leash before it could spool away from her.

"Tray was talking about taking a dog for a run, he can take Shadow with him," Toren said, half-dragging her from the van. "You'll love it, come on! I'll get the gear."

"Will I need my coat?" she asked. She was wearing one of the old, insulated plaid flannel shirts that had been packed for her sister's van.

"You'll want gloves and a hat," Toren advised. "But I'll work you hard enough that you won't need more of a coat."

"Oo," Carina said with a grin. "I love it when you talk dirty to me."

Toren found a spare hat and gloves with the hockey sticks and soccer ball in the back of the garage and he pulled the wool hat down over Carina's eyes before he rolled it up to display the Alaska hockey league logo.

"I'm really living the princess life here," she scoffed, straightening it with a laugh. She pulled on the gloves, shouldered one of the sticks, and they went to the dog yard.

Tray, fortunately, was game for taking Shadow. "I promise I won't let him out of my sight," he swore to Carina. "I'll wear our new escape artist out on the upper trail with Dana."

Shadow looked distinctly unhappy about this arrangement, but Carina ruffled his fur and sent him away, gamely following Toren to the field behind the castle where there were already goals set up.

Toren couldn't remember the last time he'd played a simple game of one-on-one.

The rules were simple: try to get the ball in the opponent's goal, no hands, keep the stick low.

Carina played hard, and cheated her heart out swinging her hockey stick like a bat and using both hands to wrestle the ball from him directly at one point. They laughed and ran and she shed even her light flannel.

"What's the score?" she asked when they finally stopped, gasping for breath and feeling lighter-hearted than Toren thought possible. Their breath steamed in the air as they panted.

"About a hundred to one," he told her. "You're terrible at this."

"I scored twice!" she protested. Her ears and cheeks were bright red from the cold. "Don't you take that from me!"

"You cheated!"

"You let me!"

"Are you hungry?" Toren asked, and he didn't mean food.

"So hungry," Carina replied, and she didn't mean food either.

"Grim and Amused are going to have the best stories to tell the rest of the guard tonight," Carina said, as they abandoned their equipment and ran for the castle hand-in-hand.

Toren realized he'd completely forgotten the guards were there. This was the new normal.

CHAPTER 35

The royal garage was the place that Carina felt the most comfortable. It was warm compared to the chilly outdoors, but cool compared to the castle, which was already being transformed for the impending engagement party. She could close the door and let Shadow off the leash inside; everyone knew to enter and exit carefully so he wouldn't escape. And the van was there, a promise of freedom that she couldn't quite reach.

Raval was often there, tinkering with one of the motorcycles, or rebuilding something on one of the workbenches. He was one of the middle brothers, Carina knew, and the one who could work magic. He was the only blond, and sometimes his gaze was unsettlingly direct. He didn't invite conversation, and she didn't pursue it.

"Do you have a screwdriver I could use?" she asked him cautiously, a few days after her field hockey game with Toren. "There's a cabinet door in the van that's a little loose."

Raval gave her one of those sharp looks, and nodded. "Second drawer in the tool chest."

Carina followed his gesture to a tall stack of drawers and

found a neat row of screwdrivers in dozens of sizes. "Thank you," she said. She nearly tripped over Shadow, who had followed her hopefully, and gave his ears a ruffle.

She tightened every screw she could find in the van, even the ones that didn't need it, and went to return the tool to the drawer she'd found it in.

"Thanks," she told Raval shyly. Then she screwed up her courage. "Toren said that you...work magic."

She wondered if Raval's eyes were so unsettling because they were so much like Toren's: silvery-blue, with depth like gemstones, but not nearly as *warm*.

"Yeah," Raval said unhelpfully. Then he seemed to thaw a little. "You probably have questions."

Carina chuckled. "You could say that." There was an empty stool down the workbench from him, and she perched on it. "I feel like there are things that the queen of Alaska should know."

Raval nodded solemnly. "I'm happy to explain anything I can."

"Toren told me a little," Carina said, trying to figure out where to start. The stool was on a swivel and she had to resist her urge to spin herself. That was definitely not *royal*. "He said that you have to write it down. And that it burns paper."

Raval's face was guarded, and Carina realized abruptly how much she had come to recognize Toren's expressions over the past week.

"Let me start somewhere else," he said cautiously. "When I concentrate on something really hard, I feel like I'm pushing against something, like I'm trying to squeeze something that really doesn't want to go."

"Like you're squeezing that last bit of toothpaste out of a tube?" Carina guessed. Then she realized that Raval had probably never had to squeeze out the last bit of toothpaste in his life.

To her relief, Raval laughed. "Yes, exactly like that. And if you don't have a place for that toothpaste to go, there's a terrible mess. So I have to channel it all into words, broken down into letters, and the act of writing it down sort of locks it into place and keeps the intention sort of poised there until it needs to be used."

"So...you could just write down 'burn', and then you have a piece of paper you can use as a lighter?"

Raval looked horrified. "Not even a little."

Carina made herself not twist on the stool again.

He sighed. "Okay, so you've got this intention in your head, like..." he sighed *"burn*. But if you just set loose something like that, it doesn't know what, or where, or how long, though that will depend a lot on the strength of the person setting the spell, and you end up with basically that idiot holding onto fireworks in a viral video where the best possible outcome is terrible burns and humiliation. Have you ever read a really long legal contract? The kind of thing where seventeen lawyers were consulted and there's a clause for everything, even stuff that would never, ever happen? That's what you have to do with spells. If they can go wrong, they will, because magic is wild."

"Like genies," Carina said thoughtfully.

"Like...genies?"

"When you make wishes, you have to word it really carefully, or you end up buried in a pile of gold or married to a horse or a hundred years old."

Raval's mouth quirked into a reluctant smile. "Like genies. Or dealing with the fae."

The fae were real? Carina shook her head, trying not to get distracted.

"Okay, so you write out a legal document for magic. But not on paper."

"It can be on paper, if you only want it to work once. But it takes a long time to write out a good spell, so you kind of do want it to be on something that will last. I know a couple of casters who will spend a good month on one basic lock spell. It takes a lot of concentration, a lot of time, there are no shortcuts like copy machines. You have to write every single letter with intention, which takes intense concentration, and you may as well be carving it into something. The slower you go, the more power you can infuse it with. It will still *fade* with every use, but at least you get to use it more than once. Anyway, it's almost always the case that you might as well just buy a lighter, or a deadbolt, or whatever. There are almost no cases where a spell is an improvement over something mundane."

Carina absorbed that, wondering if Raval didn't sound a little sad. It occurred to her that feeling Toren's emotions had given her a tremendous edge in getting to know him. "So, how do you activate a spell?"

"That has to be defined in it somewhere. Sometimes you give it a spoken keyword, something you say to make it happen. Sometimes you can put in parameters of some kind, like when it gets wet, or when it reaches a certain temperature. When I was a kid, I used to write spells for warmth and put them in my boots. They would activate when my toes got cold." Raval looked abashed, like he'd said more than he meant to, and he turned back to what he was working on: tiny, perfect writing, scratched all over what looked like an engine part.

"What's this you're working on?" Carina asked.

"It's an experiment," Raval growled, sounding uninviting.

Carina caught herself twisting on the stool when he didn't go on and she wasn't sure how to prod him.

"So, the fae are real?" she finally asked.

Raval nodded. "Some of the stories anyway. There are elemental spirits. Did you meet Angel?"

"Angel?" Carina had met a hundred people at least, since she'd come to the palace. "No, I don't think so."

"Out at the hot springs, you might have seen a beautiful woman in the mist?"

"Oh," Carina said. "I was kind of busy at the hot springs. Fainting, and all." She blushed.

Raval chuckled. "Oh, well Angel met *you*, at least. She's a naiad, a kind of water spirit. She controls the temperature of the water. She's a kind of natural magic, like shifters."

"Are there a lot of these spirits?" Mrs. James had mentioned spirits in the castle. Carina hadn't seen one, but she wouldn't have been surprised by one at this point.

"They're rare," Raval said. "And shy. We've got one here in the palace, but we go years without seeing her."

That must be the spirit Mrs. James had mentioned. "Are there a lot of shifters?" Carina asked.

"Maybe one in a thousand people," Raval said with a shrug. "It's hard to know, because they are secretive for obvious reasons."

"Are there a lot of magic...er...casters?"

"Maybe one in ten thousand? One in a hundred thousand? Less? I only know a few, and it's more secret than shifting."

Carina found a question close to the one she really wanted to ask, hovering on her tongue. "And the Compact..."

That earned her another one of Raval's sharp looks. "The Compact is older than Alaska," he said. "It's from a time so long ago that nothing is left but mythology. We don't understand most of it, and no caster is alive now who could do anything even similar."

"You said spells fade," Carina said. "If the Compact is so

old, how is it still working?" And how did it work on *her*? she didn't quite dare ask.

"It is renewed," Raval explained. "The kings come together every hundred years with their parts of the compact and the spell is worked again."

"Their *parts*? I thought the Compact was like a contract. But I guess it can't be on paper if it's actually a spell..."

"The original Compact is on dragonskin," Raval said. "Every member of the Small Kingdoms has a part of the original, as well as a mundane paper copy."

Carina shuddered. "Dragon...skin?"

"The founder of the kingdoms sacrificed himself to set it in place, according to the stories."

"That's a little creepy," Carina said.

"It's our history," Raval said, and Carina felt like she'd just had her hand smacked.

Shadow, who was lying on the concrete floor, gave a groan, and then bolted to his feet as a door opened with a swirl of cold air at the far end of the garage.

Carina rose, leaving the stool spinning free behind her, when she recognized Mrs. James. She was undoubtedly needed for deportment lessons, or dance practice, or to check the fit of something. "Thank you," she told Raval, who was bending back to his work. He gave the barest of nods.

Her head felt so full of new information that Carina walked slowly across the floor, like it might jostle loose if she stepped carelessly.

CHAPTER 36

"Did you have fun at school today?" Carina asked, as she curtsied to Toren under the watchful eyes of the dance instructor. She was wearing heels, because she needed the practice not only walking, but especially dancing in them. She was wearing her striped tights, though, and a large sweater with holes in the elbows.

Toren bowed to her and offered his hand. "I got an A plus in applying royal seals and repeating my lines. You?"

"A minus in keeping my mouth shut and C plus in keeping my eye rolls to a minimum. I completely flunked the 'don't yawn during the droning speeches' practice, but I learned some tricks for not *looking* like I'm yawning."

Toren chuckled and pulled her into a dance position. Carina had been cramming on all the ballroom techniques, as well as a crash course on curtsies and polite small talk.

While she had been covering those things, Toren had been studying, non-stop, until his head felt like it would explode from all the history and civics he was shoving in. Rian had provided him with the tax codes and public works financial records, but that had required a simpler book on what all the words even meant. Carina had helped him understand the accounts, marveling with him over how much went into keeping a country solvent.

"Wait until you see the dress they're lacing me into," Carina said, keeping her chin up as the music started and she stepped into the dance with him. "You won't even recognize me."

"I would recognize you in anything," Toren assured her. "Even if you wore a mask."

"Oh, a masked ball!" Carina exclaimed. "I always dreamed of one of those. Is it too late to change the theme of the engagement party?" She started to step the wrong way, then corrected herself and gracefully regained her balance.

"Do you really think that Captain Luke would let anyone in wearing a *mask?*" Toren scoffed. "We're lucky she's letting the actual guests in here, and you'd better believe she's going to insist on being able to see everyone. At all times."

He regretted his flippancy at once, because Carina's face fell at the reminder of the danger they were in, and the next few steps were done grimly. He turned her, danced a few steps away and then back, and said softly, "I'm so sorry, Carina."

Her eyes were too bright when she looked back at him. "For what?"

"For all of this. For trapping you into being a queen. For putting your life in danger. For forcing you into this position. You ought to have choices, to have control of your own life and destiny, not be a pawn in old political magic."

Her whole face softened. "Are you apologizing because I have to be a princess? Isn't that every little girl's dream?" Her voice was light and carefully teasing.

Toren braved the wrath of the dancing instructor and

drew her to a stop. "You deserve your own dreams," he said firmly. "You should choose your own future."

For a moment, Carina stared at him without speaking, then she smiled, crooked and sincere. "I sometimes think that this is where I'm supposed to be. Maybe this *is* how I meet my goals. God knows I couldn't face down Amco Bank by myself." She shot a sideways glance to the toe-tapping instructor and pulled Toren back into the steps.

"I've always been powerless," she murmured. "And it's kind of exciting to think that now I could actually do good things. That I can make life better for other people. That I can fix broken systems."

"Yes," Toren agreed. "*Yes.* We can do that."

"I just have to get through curtsy lessons and finish memorizing titles and diplomats," Carina teased.

They were still smiling into each other's eyes, making a good show of dancing the approved steps, when Rian cleared his throat from the door.

"Sorry to interrupt, but I need the crown prince."

Toren laid a kiss on Carina's cheek with a sigh. "Duty calls."

"You could let it go to voicemail," she whispered back. "The van is all tuned up and full of gas..."

Toren laughed and gave her a swift embrace, then abandoned her to the sour-faced dance teacher.

Rian led him to the informal dining room. "Fask needed you to sign some things. I also wanted to let you know that Kenth sent his congratulations and an engagement gift, but regrets that he won't be attending the party. He said he'd come to the wedding."

"Does Fask already know?"

"Oh yeah. Got the *united front as a family* speech already."

"He wouldn't care if it was Raval begging off," Toren observed thoughtfully.

Rian shrugged. "You know those two," he said carelessly.

"We should fix that," Toren said.

Rian gave him a surprised glance. "You think you *can*?"

Toren gave him a crooked grin. "I'm going to be the king of Alaska. What can't I do?"

CHAPTER 37

Unlike other mornings, the castle wasn't quiet when Carina, staring sleeplessly at the ceiling, finally sat up on the morning of the engagement party. There were vehicles outside, and voices down the halls. None of it was loud enough to wake her; the thick log walls were far more soundproof than she had expected. But it was a constant undertone of sound to the murmur of anxiety in her head.

"Did you sleep?" Toren asked, sitting up with her.

"Barely," Carina admitted. "You?"

"Some."

They clung to each other for a desperate moment, then took an efficient shower that was *almost* distracting.

The original plan had been to host the engagement event at the hot springs. But the assassination attempt made Captain Luke put her foot down and insist that they have it at the castle itself, where she could monitor all the security arrangements. The wedding, she conceded, could be scheduled at the resort, once she'd had time to evaluate how best to protect the family.

Breakfast was in the informal dining room, which was

already undergoing a transformation for the engagement party. Everything was hung in gold stars and sheer blue cloth. The other rooms on the second floor were even more underway, and golden lanterns were being hung by an army of workers.

"Your make-up artist and stylist will be here at one," Mrs. James greeted her, laying a style portfolio next to her as Carina sat at the table. "We'll walk through the ceremony at three, we'll do photographs directly after, and the event itself officially starts at five."

Was the make-up artist the same person as the stylist? Carina wondered, but she didn't ask, just took the cup of coffee at her seat and sipped it carefully.

Before she could eat, Fask put a small box near her elbow. "We just have time to resize this, if it doesn't fit."

"What's that?" Toren asked.

"Mother's engagement ring."

All the brothers stopped eating.

"I didn't even think about a ring," Toren admitted.

For a moment, Carina was cross. Everything was so hurried, she'd never even gotten an official proposal, just an assumption that she'd go along with this like she was going along with everything else and she hadn't ever pressed the issue. It seemed a minor complaint against the tapestry of the chaos her life had descended into, but what if the ring was hideous?

With trembling hands, she put down her coffee and picked up the box, opening it like it might contain a snake.

To her relief, it was a simple diamond ring, with a small, sparkling jewel in a plain gold band. She slipped it on, aware of all the eyes on her.

It fit remarkably well, and was ridiculously heavy. She started to slip it off again, but Fask told her, "Leave it on, you might as well get used to wearing it."

Breakfast, as good as it was, was hard to eat and Carina was keenly aware of the weight on her finger and sparkle of it at the corner of her eye.

After breakfast, she picked hairstyles and make-up from a catalog, and chose from a selection of family jewels laid out on velvet trays. Toren disappeared with Fask, and strange people came in and out at random to measure her and fuss with decorations and frown at her hair.

When Carina finally thought she might escape, Fask came back, and spread photographs across the table before her, pointing out all the visiting royalty that she would be expected to meet. "Green and gold are the New Siberian Islands, north of Russian. They're only sending a non-noble dignitary, which is a reflection of our opinions of each other. Purple and silver are Mo'orea, tiny island near French Polynesia, the king and queen will be here. Great friends of my father."

Toren came back while she was attempting to memorize titles and looked over her shoulder. He startled, and picked up one of the photographs.

"Teal and silver," Carina recited, practicing her smile at him. "Island of Majorca in the Mediterranean Sea. They're sending... um..."

"This is the man who was staring at you at the hot springs," Toren said, and everyone around them froze. "The man I saw again at the festival."

"Are you *sure*?" Fask asked.

"Positive."

Carina gazed at the photograph as a murmur of speculation rose around them. She groped for Toren's hand and held it so hard that the unfamiliar ring cut into her finger.

"He would certainly know how badly Alaska needs a succession to happen before the Renewal," Toren suggested.

Fask nodded grimly. "Drayger is one of six bastard sons

and the king of Majorca has three legitimate children before you even get to those. He's got some kind of paper title—baronet, maybe?—but his chances of inheriting land are nothing on that postage stamp. If Alaska is carved into colonies, he'd have a shot at something worth having. Our enemies would be very generous with the man responsible for the conquest of Alaska." He frowned at Carina. "If either one of you dies before the coronation, we're screwed."

"No pressure," Toren muttered as the rest of the room exploded into speculation and suggestions.

"Never mind one of us *dying*," Carina murmured in reply.

But Fask was already walking away, speaking into an earpiece. He was undoubtedly ordering more guards and security. Captain Luke was going to have *kittens*.

Her breakfast like a brick in the bottom of her stomach, Carina finished committing the most important of the visiting dignitaries to memory.

CHAPTER 38

Toren had weathered many parties like this one, but they had always been parties with other people in focus. This was the first event where he was the headliner, the one in the spotlight, and he distinctly didn't enjoy it.

Carina, he noticed at once, was a natural.

She was a shining star in the blue dress that had been tailored to match Toren's uniform. The huge skirt was shimmering blue material in a dozen filmy layers. The bodice was solid blue with blue embroidery all over it. Gold stars were subtly tucked into the swirls. It had little cap sleeves, and a modest neckline that showed just a tease of Carina's cleavage. She had complained bitterly about having to wear heels, but agreed that her hiking boots didn't exactly complete the image.

She smiled and nodded and was shy and bold in exactly the right measures. She remembered everyone's titles and her simple charm and sweet smile set everyone around her at ease.

Her sister, June, and her big, quiet boyfriend didn't exactly fit in with the rest of the royal and royal-adjacent crowd, but they had good manners and followed their coaching with enthusiastic good will, bowing or curtseying only a little too much.

"Are they going to live with us here?" Toren asked, when conversation drew him a little away with Carina.

"You can't put June and I in the same house," Carina warned. "Not even one this big. I talked to Mrs. James about putting them up in town somewhere. I guess you have some nice properties? June's even talking about Anchorage. She wants to see a little more before settling down. Are you sure that's not an... imposition? To put them up?"

"It's no trouble," Toren promised. "Family of yours is family of mine."

"She'll probably go nuts without some work after a few months, she's like me that way. She's talking about volunteering somewhere. Maybe something with kids."

They were interrupted by the king and queen of Mo'orea then, and made idle conversation about trade agreements and family. "Our daughter wanted to come," the king said off-handedly. "She's always wanted to visit Alaska."

"Our house is always open for her," Carina said, before Toren could.

Toren added, "I think Carina would appreciate company that wasn't six loud brothers."

"She can be loud," the queen laughed. "I think she would like you," she said to Carina. "You've been very brave and we're all pulling for you right now."

It was as close as they came to talking about Carina's charges and criminal troubles. Not all the guests were that polite about the topic, casting curious looks at Carina, and asking questions that she neatly sidestepped.

Dinner was a lengthy affair, complete with stage entertainment.

Fask gave a heartfelt speech that managed to be

completely *factual* and not address any of the driving questions that all the guests clearly had.

Toren stood, with Carina, at the end of the speech and they smiled at each other. Toren thanked everyone with a few brief words, and then dessert was served in the other room, where people could circulate and network. He wondered if he should have insisted on making the main speech, but was happy just to be grateful for one less thing to do.

Toren could see Carina flagging as the night went on, her smile growing more forced and her glances at Toren more desperate. He found himself playing interference more and more often, and he was not the slightest bit surprised when he looked up from a conversation with the dignitary from the New Siberian Islands about obscure hockey regulations to find that she was gone.

CHAPTER 39

Carina knew that the guards weren't far behind, and she felt bad for leaving Toren to deal with their festivities by himself, but her mind was too busy for more idle chit-chat, more vacant smiles and more repeats of 'It's classified,' and 'I'm afraid I'm not supposed to talk about that.'

The ring was heavy on her finger, and she twisted it anxiously on her finger as she crept out. She'd gotten turned around in the halls, and where she'd meant to come out at the dog kennels where Shadow was under lock and key, she was on the side of the castle now, overlooking the wide lawn where she and Toren had played field hockey.

She didn't actually try to run away, though the temptation was strong. She just leaned against one of the massive log porch columns, and then slid to a seat as she realized that there wasn't enough strength in her legs to hold her up.

The fabric of her skirt crinkled as it folded around her in a nest of shimmery blue.

Grim and Amused burst out of the door, spotted her, and sedately retreated into an out of the way position at the far end of the porch as if she had never been out of their sight. One of them touched their ear and murmured something.

She should find June, Carina thought. Make sure that she and her boyfriend were settling in, *safe*.

But right now, it was quiet outside compared to the noisy, bright din of the party, and quite dark. The sky above was deep blue, with glittering stars barely visible against the interference of the light from the porch. Most of the leaves had already fallen from the bare birches, and the evergreens were dark sentinels of the forest around. There was a wide yard between the castle and the edge of the woods; Carina had first thought it was just for show, but considering it now, she realized that it was also a very convenient place to land visiting dragons, as well as an excellent lawn for field hockey.

There was an arc of color in the sky, a smudge of green and purple, and Carina's first thought was that she was seeing a faint aurora. Then it resolved itself into exactly one of the dragons she'd been considering, circling dark over the velvety sky, blotting out the stars as it grew near.

It didn't escape the notice of the guards, who stopped even trying to be in the background and came to flank her. One of them was talking into their earpiece as the dragon back-winged to a landing that whipped Carina's skirts into a flurry as the other took her arm and helped her to her feet without leaving it an option.

But before they could get her back into the castle, the dragon was shifting and calling out, "Carina Andresen, I have something you need!"

Carina recognized him at once; this was, without doubt, Drayger, the bastard son from Majorca.

Both her guards had guns out now, trained on the intruder. She could hear shouts from inside the castle, and there were more guards running from around the sides of the castle.

But Carina was staring at what Drayger was holding aloft.

It was a flash drive, the colors of Amco Bank clear even in the muted light from the porch.

"Wait," she said, a hand on the arm of the nearest guard.

"I'll treat with the princess," Drayger shouted. "Or this gets destroyed!" He held it between his fingers, and no one could doubt that he was capable of crushing it in his fist.

"I'm not a princess yet," Carina shouted back, not offering to close the distance between them. "Where did you get that?"

He remained where he was, not testing the resolve of the several dozen men and women who now had him dead to sights.

Did bullets kill dragons? Carina suddenly wondered. He was certainly doing his best to keep his hands up and look unthreatening.

Except that her evidence, her *freedom*, was on that flash drive.

"I'm not here to hurt you!" he called firmly.

"Then why the hell *are* you here?" Carina demanded. "And where did you get that flash drive?"

That was when Toren dropped from the second story porch, pouncing in dragon shape and seizing Drayger in wicked claws.

"He's got my flash drive!" Carina cried, and Toren froze with his claws flexed against Drayger's flesh. A thin trickle of blood stained his white shirt; he looked like he was dressed for a party.

Their party.

Drayger, to everyone's surprise, did not shift into a dragon to battle Toren, only hung limply in his claws with his arms raised in truce.

"I'm not here to hurt you!" he repeated.

Toren shifted, stepped forward, and swiftly punched him in the face. "You shot my mate!" he snarled.

Drayger's hands were still up, spread except for his grip on the drive. He took Toren's blow and staggered back to balance. "I didn't shoot your mate," he snarled back just as fiercely.

"Me, then?" Toren hissed.

Drayger shook his head, lowering his hands slowly. "I didn't shoot either one of you. I didn't even shoot *at* you. I'm a crack shot and if I'd wanted either one of you dead, you *would* be. I put that bullet right in the window where I wanted it."

No one knew what to do. The guards by Carina had drawn up their weapons when Toren entered the fray, not willing to accidentally shoot the crown prince.

Slowly, carefully, Drayger wound up and tossed the drive at Carina, who stepped forward in her swishing skirts to catch it, the guards still flanking her.

If it wasn't her drive, it was a perfect replica, with the same scratched corner.

"Is the data still on this?" she challenged.

"I didn't touch it," Drayger promised.

"Can you check?" Toren asked, looking rather like he wanted to deck Drayger again just for the fun of it.

"Not without Amco Bank's proprietary decryption software," Carina said apologetically, holding the drive tight in her fist. "Which is part of how it's good proof. How did you get this?"

Drayger smiled rakishly. "To be honest, I was casing the castle, flying overhead, and I saw an intruder cutting the camera wires. I was curious, followed him into the garage, and caught him lifting it from your van. I figured it was important, stashed in the headlight like that."

"Who could have known where it was?" Carina wondered out loud.

"I'm not done with the shooting at us part," Toren protested. "Why did you do it? Why were you following us? Because the reasons I can think of don't include 'saving us from theft out of the goodness of your heart'. You stand to gain a lot from a broken Alaska."

Drayger's smile cooled. "That's why they approached me."

"They?" Carina and Toren spoke together.

"We should speak privately," Drayger suggested, his gaze raking the audience that was starting to gather.

CHAPTER 40

Toren still wanted to punch Drayger. He wasn't done with wanting justice for being shot at and terrified for Carina this last week.

"Majorca wants Alaska to fall." Fask had taken control of the meeting, of course.

"Who doesn't want Alaska to fall?" Drayger countered. "By pure dumb luck, you six have your claws on some of the richest lands in the world, and while the Compact protects you, no one can do anything about that." He didn't seem bothered by the scrutiny of five brothers and Carina, or the handful of guards flanking him. Captain Luke looked like she was a wrong word away from personally wringing his neck.

"I don't know who *these* specific players are," he admitted. "My contact is just a middleman. He said he represented a coalition of interested parties and…he made me a very tempting offer."

He continued confidently, "You aren't the only ones who've studied the Compact and figured out how to get you out of it. Plenty of people know your father is in a coma and unlikely to survive. And plenty of those same people know that if one of you finds a mate, you can take his throne. It doesn't take a high degree of intelligence to figure out that if you take out the mates, you take out Alaskan sovereignty."

"Are they responsible for our father's state?" Rian demanded.

"I don't know that," Drayger replied to Rian.

"You shot at Carina," Toren could not help saying.

"I gave a good show of shooting at Carina," Drayger corrected. "I was hired to kill her, but I...couldn't. I'm a soldier, not a murderer, and I'm not going to sell my soul. Not for land, not for anything."

"Did you change your mind *while* you were shooting at us?" Carina demanded.

"I shot near you," Drayger scoffed. "Just close enough to cause a scene. Get into the papers, thank you for having the press on hand, by the way. I made it look like I was trying, and gave myself an excuse to stay low. If I'd really wanted to kill you, I could have poisoned you at the hot springs in a hot minute." For the first time, he looked abashed and uncertain. "On this topic...I'd like to apply for asylum."

The room silenced.

"I'd have to check our treaty with Majorca, but that's probably the kind of asylum we *could* actually grant," Rian said thoughtfully. "It fits the usual restrictions."

"You want us to grant you asylum because you were hired to kill our crown prince's mate and you've had a crisis of conscience?" Fask's dry voice was perfect for the moment and Toren made a mental note to learn how to use it.

"Why didn't you come forward sooner?" Tray asked suspiciously.

"Would you have listened?" Drayger retorted. "I waited until I had some leverage."

Everyone looked at the flash drive sitting on the table between them.

"But you didn't use it as leverage," Carina said softly. "You just gave it to me."

"A gesture of goodwill," Drayger said carelessly. Toren thought that his easy pose was just that: a pretense to cover his anxiousness.

"Who was stealing it from the van?" Toren asked. "How would *they* know it was there?"

"It was a red-headed man with a kind of a weasel-y look to him," Drayger said. "No one I knew, no convenient name tag or business card. I asked him some questions he refused to answer, and when I started to insist, we had a...struggle. I hurt his wrist, he dropped the flash drive, and we heard guards coming. He fled on foot, I went on wing. I lost sight of him in the trees."

No one could identify the mysterious thief from that description.

"We'll circle back to him," Fask said. "Let's deal with one criminal at a time."

"I've read the stories about Miss Andresen's problems with the law, and given the hiding place of the drive, I guessed that the flash drive was an important part of her defense." Drayger gave Carina a long look. "Amco Bank is not a small enemy, my lady."

Carina gave a dry laugh.

"I don't trust this guy," Rian said flatly.

"Does it count as asylum if we put him in prison?" Tray suggested dryly.

"This isn't a lot to build a relationship..." Fask started.

"Wait."

Toren didn't realize that he'd spoken until he heard the words, and everyone's attention was on him. "Those guys still think you're working for them."

Drayger shrugged. "You're still alive, so I must not be very serious about it."

"But they don't know that. Your contacts...all they know is that there was an attempt, someone that matches your description in the news. You've gone to ground, for all they know. It would be smart to lay low for a little while after something that public. They don't know you've changed loyalties."

"Not wanting to kill a few innocent people isn't the same as changing loyalties," Rian cautioned.

But Drayger knew where Toren was going. "You want me to be a double agent," he said shrewdly.

Fask scowled, considering. "The guards all knew we had identified him, they had his photo to screen guests."

"All the more reason to excuse the fact that he hasn't made another attempt," Toren said. "If they still think he's working for them, we can get more information, and we can feed them information we want them to have."

"Like...?"

Toren's spy movie knowledge failed him. "Like...um..."

Carina swept to his rescue. "Rian is researching a way to selectively activate a mate bond. Tell them that you've already figured out a way to do this for each of the brothers. Trying to stage the death of one prince is not at all the same thing as having to kill off the entire line."

Toren took a certain amount of satisfaction in the dumbfounded looks over his brothers' faces.

"The Compact usually only taps one mate per kingdom," Drayger said patiently.

"I thought no one actually understood how the Compact worked," Carina replied evenly. "And usually isn't always."

Drayger actually laughed. "You are truly becoming a savvy politician, princess."

"I'm not technically a princess yet," Carina reminded him. "This is just an engagement party."

"There is more to royalty than empty titles," Drayger told her.

"There is more to loyalty than empty words," Carina countered.

"I will pass on any information you request me to," Drayger agreed with an admiring nod at Carina. "And I will bend my knee to the crown of Alaska." He kept his gaze on Carina, to Toren's mixed annoyance and pride. He appreciated that Drayger recognized Carina's power and cleverness, but was jealous of his obvious interest in her.

"We'll discuss what information we'll choose to pass along," Fask said sharply. "I'm sure you will understand if we keep you under guard."

Luke gave a growl.

"Perfectly understandable," Drayger agreed, with a glance at the Captain. "But I will require the return of my phone in order to make contact with my handlers."

"Under supervision," Fask conceded. "For now, we will treat you as an honored guest. We'll even give you one of the third floor guest rooms with a view of the mountains. Nothing but our best."

"Testing my loyalty?" Drayger guessed. "I assure you, I very much look forward to a quiet time enjoying the *view*."

"Oh, I assure you, we have other protections in place. We aren't trusting your loyalty *that* far." Fask turned to his brothers. "I'll get the flash drive into our vault. The continued absence of half the royal family is going to be noticed at the engagement party." He gave Carina an unexpected half-smile. "If you mussed your hair and went back with Toren, the reason for *your* disappearance would be obvious."

Everyone chuckled, except the guards, and Tray and Rian slipped out of the room. Toren took Carina's hand into his elbow and walked out with her into the hallway. She sagged against him as soon as the door closed behind them.

"We've got your flash drive again," Toren told her, slipping his arm up around her shoulder to pull her close. "We've got all the cards. We know who shot at us, and why, and it won't happen again. It's all going to be alright. You're safe."

"I know," she murmured into his shoulder. "I know."

"I think Fask had the right idea," Toren suggested. Her lithe body up close against him made him forget the tangled problems of politics and trust. She was all he needed in the world.

"About keeping Drayger under guard?" Carina asked, pulling away to eye him quizzically.

"About mussing your hair," Toren said, and it was the first time since their hockey game that his grin felt truly natural.

CHAPTER 41

There was no point in messing up her hair with her own hands, so Carina let Toren thread his fingers into her updo and pull her into a kiss full of hope and promise. Relief and happiness flooded through her.

Carina hadn't ever spent a lot of time imagining her perfect wedding or designing her wedding gown or mooning over cute boys. She had pictured a long, single life as a boring accountant, married only to her work. Maybe she'd get a dog.

And when her life had toppled upside down, marriage was the last thing on her mind. Even when she was forced into the arrangement, it seemed like a formality, just a title, just a name for a business transaction that was in everyone's best interests.

But something had changed, over the last week. Underneath her magical attraction, underneath her need for his protection, underneath all the pressure from every angle, Carina found herself more and more fond of Toren. He was her best friend, always in her corner, constantly picking her up and reminding her of her own strengths.

She would have agreed to marry Toren even if he hadn't been a dragon shifter and a prince. She would have married him if he'd been a pauper, or one of the crazy Alaskan sourdoughs with a beard to his knees.

She would have married him even without the mate magic, Carina realized, kissing him until she was breathless and dizzy.

It wasn't *just* that she felt irresistibly drawn to him anymore. If that compulsion were suddenly to go away, she would still love him.

The thought drew her up short and her lips froze.

She *loved* this man, this sweet, funny, clever prince of Alaska.

"Are you okay?" Toren asked, because of course he would. Carina stared into his silver eyes and wanted his infatuation with her to be real more than anything else in the whole world.

Tears flooded her own eyes. "Yes," she said faintly. "Yes, of course. Everything is working out at last."

"You've been so amazing and strong," Toren said, stroking his fingers along her cheek. She could feel that some of her hair had come loose and was tickling at her neckline.

"*You've* been amazing," she echoed.

"Yes, yes, you're both amazing," Fask said, coming up silently behind them. "That is very appropriately mussed hair, now let's get back to your party, lovebirds."

His smile as he passed them was tolerant and fond and Toren and Carina both beamed at each other foolishly.

Toren tucked a stray lock back in and declared her perfect.

Carina took his hand and felt strong enough to return to the sea of nobility and diplomats, with their prying eyes and all the questions she couldn't answer.

The floor had been cleared for dancing when they

returned, and no one seemed to wonder where they had been or why Carina would prefer to float around in the strong arms of her fiancé prince to socializing.

They spent the rest of the evening with each other, dancing and deflecting questions in duet, until the guests gradually left and Fask finally dismissed them with a nod to trudge wearily back to their rooms, Carina's hated shoes in her hands.

"Carina..." Toren said at the door as they left the guards behind.

"I'm trying to decide if I'm too tired for a shower before bed," Carina admitted. Her scalp felt stiff with unfamiliar product, and she ought to at least scrub off the layers of make-up or it would be all over the pillow in the morning. She'd probably break out, too, and that would be very un-princess-y of her.

When she looked longingly at the bed, Toren took her hand and led her past, to the bathroom, where he turned on the hot water and slowly undressed her.

She had not expected to have the energy to want him that night, but every touch set her skin on fire. He tenderly pulled every jewel from her upswept hair, gem by gem, and combed through it with his fingers until it was soft and loose again, letting his hands just linger on her bare shoulders and arms as he did.

Steam rose from the shower, giving the bathroom a surreal feel on the tail of a very surreal day indeed. Then he opened the door and drew her into the hot water and she tipped her face up and let it spill over her.

In a few moments, he joined her, and they soaped each other gently, finding all the places that made each other hiss and moan. His cock was firm and focused, and it filled her hand as she soaped his balls. He washed her back and kissed her soapy neck and even carefully washed the make-up from her face, smiling at her tenderly as she trustingly opened her eyes at the end.

They made slow love in the bathroom, in a nest of towels, before moving to the bed, where Toren lay her down and drove into her, urgent and patient all at once.

He was perfect and princely and Carina didn't want to sleep afterwards, because it all felt like a dream that would vanish when she woke.

CHAPTER 42

Carina was gone when Toren finally opened his eyes. The night's events flooded back as he sat up. The flash drive. Drayger's change of allegiance. The party, and the sea of dignitaries who might be involved in hiring to kill them. Carina.

He sat up with a sigh.

It was late in the morning, and low fall sunlight spilled in through open curtains.

"Oh good, you're up."

Mrs. James came bustling out of the bathroom with an armful of the towels that Toren was pretty sure they'd left on the floor the night before. She didn't scold him for leaving them there, or flicker an eyelid at the nudity he quickly hid under his blankets. "Fask wants you in his office as soon as you've eaten. You've missed breakfast, so you can feed yourself in the kitchen because no one is going to wait on you hand and foot *today*."

"Thank you, Mrs. James."

"Thank yourself," she said tartly in return on her way out.

Toren dressed quickly and wandered out into the

common area. Carina was sitting with Fask at the dais. Shadow, who had been allowed back into the house now that the party was over, was sitting next to her, leaning his big head on her knee while she scratched his ears. Carina had also selected the chair to Fask's right, Toren noted, not their father's throne. There had already been considerable discussion about the size and position of Carina's chair.

"Fask was going to show me the vault," Carina said. "To put my mind at ease."

Shadow's ears swiveled forward and his head lifted.

Carina told him, "Vault, Shadow, not w-a-l-k."

Shadow seemed unconvinced, his thick tail swishing on the floor, and when Carina and Fask rose to their feet, he bounded to four paws and seemed ready to lead the way.

"Want me to take him out while you do that?" Toren offered.

Shadow's ears lay back and he went to Carina's other side.

"It's like he understood that," Carina laughed, patting his head. She reached for Toren's hand. "Come with me, and we'll all go for a walk afterwards."

Shadow's ears perked back up at the word 'walk.'

Fask led the way down the wide back stairs, dismissing the guards. There was clearance for a dragon, if it folded its wings in and was careful of the railings.

It wound down into the caverns beneath the castle, and Carina walked closer to Toren the further they went, Shadow at her other side.

The walls turned to solid stone, beautiful granite catching the intermittent lights.

"I've heard of dragon hoards," Carina said nervously as the floor leveled and the sound of their steps echoed back at them. Shadow's claws on the floor were particularly loud. "But to be honest, I didn't think of you guys actually having one. When you said vault, I assumed...a big wall safe or something."

"It is much more secure than that," Fask assured her.

They stopped at a door to the side of the hall, approximately ten feet tall and unassumingly made of wood. It was covered from top to bottom in words, and sizzled with structured magic. No battering ram could break this door, no army could breach it.

Fask put his hand flat against it and spoke his full name before Toren could. "Faskritranum."

The door cracked open, and when Fask pushed, it swung soundlessly in.

"Oh," Carina said on an inhale. "Oh, I see."

Beyond the door was the hoard.

Toren honestly found it a little tacky and preferred the austere wealth of the public floors. This hoard was classic dragon treasure—piles of coins and collections of golden goblets and crowns and strings of pearls and exquisite necklaces and stacks of silver bracelets and copper trunks of rings. Each of the brothers had their own alcove of treasure —partly inherited and partly gathered. Fask's was rather impressive, but most of the other brothers had followed other pursuits. Rian's was mostly rare books and antique bottles. Raval had shelves of rare, sealed action figures mixed in with structured magic items. Toren found that he was a weird combination of reluctant and eager to show Carina his own modest collection of art and gold treasures. Would she care that he had one of Wayne Gretzky's Stanley Cup winning hockey sticks?

All of them together paled with their father's central hoard, heaped high with priceless treasures.

Carina nodded, walking into the room slowly with Shadow at her side. "Thank you," she said, and her voice was rich in meaning.

"Once these doors are closed, no one can get in but one of us," Toren explained. Carina's hand in his squeezed.

"Here," Fask said, leading them in through a maze of treasure. The flash drive looked out of place on the display table near the center. "There is no place in the world that is safer for this." He pointed out some of the other items on the table.

There were fine antique watches, some of the earliest ever made, a bracelet carved from a single emerald, a black ceremonial dagger in a stand etched all over with magic writing, crystal goblets, a fragile antique vase. The Compact was under glass, the paper copy next to the thick, dragonskin original pages that were in their care.

Carina picked up the dagger curiously. Fask and Toren both drew back. "Careful with that," Toren said.

"This is that knife you told me about," Carina guessed, putting it down swiftly. "The one that's spelled to kill dragons. Sorry."

Toren was so busy watching her face, embarrassment that he couldn't sense, but still recognized, flashing over her features, that he didn't notice Shadow at first.

Fask was standing at the far end of the display table. Carina stood before the table, Toren on one side, Shadow on the other, and by the time he fully realized that Shadow was changing, it was too late.

In one smooth, slithering motion, Shadow was standing as a red-haired man dressed in black at Carina's side. The blue and gold collar hung loosely around his neck, the leash still in Carina's hands.

Everyone was still startling as he dived forward and snatched the flash drive in one hand and the dagger in the other. In one fluid move, he had looped the arm with the dagger over Carina's neck, holding the blade to her throat.

"No closer, dragon brothers," he hissed. "Or she loses her lifeblood right here and now."

Toren froze and was distantly aware of Fask doing the same.

"Shadow?" Carina cried. "I don't understand."

He dropped the flash drive into a pocket and grinned at Toren. "Women can't resist a cute dog, can they?"

Carina struggled, then stopped, whimpering, as Shadow drew a line of blood at her throat with the razor sharp dagger. Even if it wasn't spelled to poison a human, it was sharp enough to slit her throat.

"You're my ticket out of here," he told her, his mouth entirely too close to Carina's ear for Toren's taste. "I don't want to have to hurt you. Yet."

"Who are you?" Toren demanded. His heart hammered in his chest and he watched the blood well along the cut on Carina's skin in horror. "What do you want with the flash drive?"

"I like the name Shadow," the man said, baring his teeth in a smile. "You can call me that. Amco Bank hired me to take care of their little problem. Follow her, find out what she knows, tear her throat out in her sleep once the flash drive is disposed of and I've verified there is no copy. It would have all been much easier if you hadn't been dragged out into the spotlight." That last was to Carina, his lips almost touching the side of her face.

She gave a keen of terror.

Toren's dragon raged in his chest.

"Don't you hurt her," Toren snarled desperately. "Not one hair on her head."

"That's a possibility," Shadow said smoothly. "If I leave in one piece with the flash drive, no one else has to get hurt. This can be a perfectly civilized negotiation. We get the drive, my employer doesn't have to worry about further problems. Carina's complications go away. You get your precious queen of Alaska."

"It's a reasonable arrangement," Fask said slowly. "We're reasonable people."

"We made a copy," Carina gasped, and Toren could hear the undertone of anger to her voice. She had no intention of letting them get away with this. "When we got the drive back, we made a copy."

Fask hissed at her, but Carina bluffed boldly on. "We made a copy and we've already sent it to the newspaper with a full reveal. That was our plan the whole time. We mailed it to the Alaska Times. The whole story will be spread across Alaska by tomorrow."

Toren almost choked. The Alaska Times had a circulation of approximately four hundred and was only published monthly, but Carina wouldn't know that. Fortunately, neither did Shadow.

The assassin growled in displeasure. "That was stupid," he said, in a low cold voice. "Because now I have no reason to keep you alive at the end of this."

CHAPTER 43

Carina felt like her blood was boiling in her veins, like she was filled with helpless rage and betrayal. She'd trusted Shadow, taken him in and *loved* him. But he'd been sent to kill her, to finish destroying the life that Amco Bank had stolen from her, to cover up their terrible deeds and epic theft.

The fine line he'd cut on her throat itched as the blood there slowly dried, and she cast desperately for something to do. She met Toren's eyes and could see the fury there. *Don't do anything rash,* she thought at him with all her might. The knife at her throat might hurt her, but it would *kill* him, and she couldn't face that future.

"You need me alive to get out of here in one piece," she said in a trembling voice. "If I'm dead, there's nothing to keep them from toasting you alive on your way out." It suddenly occurred to her that she didn't know if dragons actually breathed fire. Probably, if she didn't know, Shadow didn't either.

"Apparently, though only a dragon prince can open the door, anyone can close it, and I've got just the magic to lock it against you from the outside." Shadow said darkly to Fask and Toren. "Her Highness and I are going to walk right out of here."

"I'm not a princess yet," Carina muttered automatically. She was still holding Shadow's leash in her hands; he didn't seem to even notice the blue and gold collar hanging loose at his neck. She kept her grip on it loose and her hands at her side and tried not to bring attention to it, hoping she'd have an opportunity to use it later. He was also handling the dagger gingerly. As a dog, he'd been limping slightly on one of his front legs. He'd let the vet do very embarrassing things to him, she realized; he'd been very thorough about embracing his role.

Drayger had scuffled with him and he'd dropped the drive, she remembered. He'd hurt Shadow's wrist in the conflict. Carina felt like she was on the edge of an idea.

Shadow shifted his grip on her. "You're close enough to a princess to get me past any guards we might meet," he said.

Carina saw Toren shifting on his feet, growling helplessly as Shadow pressed the blade against her neck a little harder.

They backed away together. Carina briefly considered going limp, or yanking on the leash, but she could only see that ending badly if Toren decided that was a cue to be heroic. She didn't want him to be killed trying to save her.

No, she wasn't willing to risk Toren, not with Shadow's hands on the deadly knife. She could get Shadow out of the room, save Toren from doing something stupid and suicidal and...

Then she was in the cool, dark hallway and Shadow was drawing the door shut. He had what looked like a shipping label covered in tiny writing that he peeled off and stuck to the door. It sizzled, and started to blacken around the edges.

She heard a muffled cry of rage from the other side of the door, and then flame flickered around the frame. Something impacted the other side with a tremendous thump, but the door didn't even shudder.

"That won't hold them long," Shadow said, and he took Carina's arm and dragged her at a half-run down the stone hall.

There were no guards in the stone hallway, to Carina's chagrin, and none at the top of the stairs. Of course not. What could possibly be safer than being with both Fask *and* Toren in their great castle basement?

For the first time, she was resentful of the fact that the castle wasn't bustling with people the way she'd always imagined a castle would be. Last night, it had been impossible to round a corner without running into a guest, or the help, but they were almost all temporary hires, and the guests had been put up in hotels and resorts nearby. Where were Grim and Amused when she could actually use them? But they were rarely shadowing her when she was with Toren within the castle, only when she was alone, or they were outside.

They walked through empty halls, their footsteps loud as they crossed the grand foyer.

"My van," Carina said desperately. "It's out front, at the end of the drive. It's really nondescript. You'll get further with it than you will stealing one of their fancy cars."

"You seem like a smart girl," Shadow observed, pulling her towards the front of the house. "Why'd you get go and get yourself mixed up in something like this? You must have known that you'd never have a chance against something like Amco Bank and the important people who own it."

"I thought I was doing the right thing," Carina said quietly. "Just because they are big or important doesn't mean they should get away with *murder*. Why would you get involved in something so unethical?"

"I've got a pack to think of," Shadow growled.

They paused just inside the front doors while Shadow

frowned at the guards standing on the porch through the repaired glass panels. They were looking away, and after a moment of considering, Shadow simply snarled and dragged Carina with him through the doors, the dagger pressed threateningly at her neck.

"Stay back and keep your hands up and she won't be hurt!" he shouted, and the guards fell back dutifully and put their hands up.

"Where's the van?" he asked Carina through clenched teeth.

The van was actually around the back of the castle in a garage. "It's down past that delivery truck," Carina lied. "You have to get out further to see it."

They maneuvered slowly down the stairs, Shadow keeping the guards in his field of view as he hauled her down each step.

Carina closed her eyes, hoped that the slim chance she was grasping at would pay off, and screamed as loud as she could.

For a long moment, nothing happened, and she was sure that she had misjudged everything. Shadow started to relax.

The sound of shattering glass was her cue, and at that moment, she tightened her grip on the leash in her hand, yanking down as hard as she could. "Bad dog!" she shouted, and a black dragon dropped out of the sky onto them.

CHAPTER 44

Toren battered himself against the locked door until Fask's yelling finally penetrated his fog of rage.

"You can't open it from in here," his brother snarled, as Toren shifted back and curled fists at his side. "He's put a one-way lock spell on it. We'll have to wait until someone opens it from the outside."

Toren couldn't resist giving the door one final kick and then he paced, tripping over the heaps of the hoard that he'd knocked over when he had shifted and charged the door. "If he hurts her…"

"He's going to keep her safe until he's sure she's not any use to him," Fask said coldly. "And that was a dumbass move, trying to bluff her way out of this mess instead of taking a perfectly logical compromise."

Of course she wouldn't compromise, Toren thought, his chest tight with worry and fear even while he felt overwhelming pride for her. Even with her life in danger, she was determined to do the right thing. She was better than any of them deserved.

Our mate! his dragon wailed in his head. *She's in danger! We must save her!*

I don't know how, Toren agonized.

"Toren, little brother, it's not your fault."

"It *is* all my fault," Toren raged. "Everything is my fault. I'm supposed to be a *king*, and I can't even keep my mate safe. I'm terrible at *everything*."

To his surprise, Fask caught his arm and pulled him into swift, heartfelt hug. "You're doing *fine*, little brother."

Surprise chased away Toren's worries for a moment.

Fask released him, and continued, "You stepped up, and it's impressed everyone. You've taken it seriously, worked hard, and been smart and diplomatic. You would have been a king that Alaska could be proud of. That I'm proud of."

Toren had craved his biggest brother's approval since he was a child. But now that he had it, it didn't matter to him. Nothing mattered but Carina, in the clutches of Shadow, being used as a hostage.

He returned to the door, prepared to batter through it with human fists if he had to, when he heard something on the other side, a crackling sound and the most wonderful thing he'd ever heard, Rian saying his own name.

"Prianriakist!"

The lock spell cracked beneath the stronger magic of the door and before Rian could even move aside, Toren was shifting and shoving his way past his brothers, surging down the hall after his mate.

He couldn't fly in the confines of the castle, but he could run, in the fast, humping gait of his dragon form, claws cutting into the wooden floor as he desperately made a beeline out the open front door for Carina, praying it wasn't too late.

He arrived in time to see a hail of broken glass fall from

above as Carina yanked down on the leash that was still around Shadow's neck.

He glance up to see Drayger in his dragon form, struggling and suspended above them in a net of shining thread, a spell activated by the breaking glass; the third floor guest room had always been intended for diplomatic visitors of uncertain loyalty.

Shadow, surprised by the hail of shards and Carina's sudden struggle, quickly recovered, but Carina was already fighting hard. She had dropped the leash to concentrate on the hand holding the deadly dagger. "Stay back!" she cried to Toren. "It's too dangerous!"

Toren had no intention of hanging back, and charged down the stairs with a roar of challenge.

Carina fought harder for the dagger, hanging on his injured wrist, but Shadow was larger and stronger, and every bit as determined. He roared in pain, but dragged Carina in an arc and Toren had to leap back as the assassin lashed out with the obsidian blade, snarling and circling. Carina stomped on his foot and elbowed him as she tried to pull down on his arm. The leash snapped loose around them.

"Don't let it touch you!" Carina begged Toren.

She and Shadow tangled together and he abruptly stopped trying to wrest free of her and drove the blade back at her with a furious slash.

Her scream of pain spurred Toren carelessly forward, and she twisted Shadow's injured wrist as she fell backwards, forcing him to drop the blade at last.

Then Shadow was standing alone, triumphant only for the moment that it took to occur to him that he no longer had a hostage *or* a magical dagger. Toren bore down on him, and the assassin shifted and tried to flee on four feet. He got no further than the drive before he was pinned beneath Toren's claws.

Toren's urge to simply shred the man was tempered only by not wishing for Carina to see him lose control, and he satisfied himself by merely throwing the man up against the statue of his grandfather, stunning him into unconsciousness and back into human form.

At the top of the steps, Fask cried out his full name and Drayger fell from the dissolved magical net, landed next to Fask, and shifted into his human shape.

Carina was sitting in a protective circle of guards with drawn guns, and there was blood staining her shirt.

"I'm okay!" she called, voice shaking. "I'm okay..."

Toren shifted, running to her.

"It's just a scratch," Carina sobbed, but she winced when Toren unbuttoned her blouse to draw the fabric back from the wound at her collarbone. It was bleeding, but didn't seem to be deep. "At least it was me and not you," she said, and she smiled bravely at Toren.

Her guards left Carina in Toren's care to secure Shadow. They weren't gentle, to Toren's satisfaction.

"The flash drive," Carina cried. "It's in his pocket!"

Shadow was briskly frisked, and one of the guards stepped back with the drive held up in his hand as the dog-shifter regained consciousness sluggishly.

"Well, that's a relief," Fask said, coming down the steps with Rian. They were both in human form. "Carina?"

"I'm okay," Carina said, drawing in a shaky breath. She clung to Toren. "I'm okay. He just got a lucky swipe in. Better me than one of you," she repeated.

Toren stripped off his shirt to wad into a makeshift bandage; Carina hissed as he applied it to her cut.

Drayger followed them and knelt beside the black dagger. He whistled, but didn't offer to pick it up. "Pretty risky having one of those around," he said.

"It was in our *vault*," Fask said crossly.

Arriving on the scene, Captain Luke stalked forward, secured the knife, and took the data drive from the guard who had retrieved it.

"Well, you aren't the only one who wants that drive," Rian said, holding out a hand to take it from the captain. "I was coming down to the vault to find you with the good news."

"I could use some good news," Fask said dryly.

"Amco Bank was already under investigation," Rian said. "I was contacted by a team from America's FBI. They've already got a warrant for the decryption software, so they'll be able to read the data and prove that it had been locked by their proprietary software. They hope to get the top executives not only on the money laundering charges, but also murder. You'd be cleared, Carina."

Carina closed her eyes and held tighter to Toren as Rian went on.

"Apparently, they already found proof that a whole lot of suspicious accounts had been deleted before they could get the key information about who had created them and who accessed them. That itself violated several policies, and would have gotten them a lot of stiff penalties and an official investigation. Carina's data is the smoking gun. It has proof of who was involved, and all the numbers they've otherwise wiped from all of their records. They're going to want this guy, too, I bet. I wonder if his fingerprints will turn anything interesting up. Like maybe something related to that murder you were accused of?"

Carina started to struggle in Toren's arms, and he quickly realized that she was trying to stand. He rose to his feet, lifting her gently with him, then let her go. She closed the distance to Shadow and everyone automatically stood at attention except him.

Shadow glared at her, hatred and frustration in his eyes

and she stared him down ferociously, one hand holding the bloody shirt to her cut shoulder.

"I trusted you," she said firmly. "I gave you a home. I gave you my last hot dogs. And you *betrayed* me. I want you to contact your employers. And I want you to tell them that the queen of Alaska doesn't negotiate with criminals, and doesn't get scared, and doesn't give up! Tell them that I am coming for them, and that I will see *all of you* brought to justice. You are a *bad dog*, and if you ever set foot in this country again, you will be put *down*."

Toren could not help grinning and he caught even the iron-faced guards doing the same. Fask looked a little nonplussed and Rian's smile was admiring. Drayger made no attempt to hide his glee, whooping with laughter.

Shadow's face grew darker and darker as he looked around at their mirth. Then he smiled himself, a humorless, teeth-baring smile. "At least I got to piss on your grandfather's statue," he snarled, and Toren gestured with his hand for the guards to take him away.

"I'll go make some phone calls," Rian said, shaking his head.

"I'll take the drive," Fask offered.

"No need," Rian said. "I'm going to transfer the data to a secure server right now."

Fask looked like he might argue, then nodded. "I'll be happy to see the end of this," he said tightly.

Carina stepped back into Toren's arms and let herself sag into his embrace. "We should get you cleaned up," he said. "You might need stitches."

Carina moved the shirt, inspecting the cut. "I doubt it," she said. "It's almost stopped bleeding."

She eyed Drayger. "I was really hoping you'd recognize him," Carina said. "And I was really, really hoping that you were looking out the window."

"It's a helluva view," Drayger said offhandedly. "And that red hair is hard to miss. You've also got excellent lungs. But I wasn't able to do much at the end."

"You distracted him," Carina pointed out. "And…it means something that you tried."

"You might have saved her," Toren said grudgingly. "Thank you."

"All my guards are gone," Drayger pointed out. Only Captain Luke remained, and she looked furious. "Shouldn't you be calling for some more to drag me back to my rooms?"

"I can drag you myself," she snarled.

Everyone looked up at the shattered window three stories above. "Mrs. James is going to have words about that," Toren observed.

"She's going to have more words about what you did to her entrance hall floor," Rian said dryly.

"We'll put you in the north-facing rooms until we can get the window replaced," Fask said thoughtfully to Drayger.

"With guards?" Drayger teased. It was clear that none of them, except possibly Captain Luke, considered him a threat any longer. He winked at her. "Want to handcuff me?"

"There are still going to be guards," Fask muttered, and they all went inside, Captain Luke keeping a particularly watchful eye on the Majorcan dragon.

CHAPTER 45

Toren took Carina to their rooms, and carefully took off her blouse, crusty with blood. It seemed like a lot of blood, for a mere human.

She felt so fragile, as he undressed her, peeling the layers of soaked fabric from her pale skin.

The cut was only barely bleeding now, the faintest stubborn ooze when he gently sponged the dried blood from her skin.

He couldn't resist kissing Carina as he worked, light kisses on her neck, at the corner of her eye.

He dried her bravely with one of Mrs. James precious white towels, and it came away clean. He daubed on antibiotic cream that he found in a cabinet, hardly daring to spread it.

Then he sat with his bride-to-be on the wide bed as she craned her head to try to see the raw gash.

"It might scar," he said, hopelessly. He had no idea how humans usually healed. "We should go to a doctor."

"I don't need a doctor," Carina scoffed. "And I don't mind a scar. It'll prove that I'm not to be messed with."

"You *aren't* to be messed with," Toren said with a crooked smile. "I always knew that. From the moment you threatened me with your camp chair."

She pulled her bra strap back up over her shoulder and would have stood to find a clean shirt, but Toren drew her back. "There's something I've been meaning to do. Something I should have done a long time ago."

"We've done *that* a bunch," Carina teased, tipping her face up for a willing kiss.

"Not that," Toren said, and Carina stilled at his seriousness.

He took a deep breath, then slipped off the bed and knelt at her feet, bowing his head and taking her hands in his own. "Carina, you've changed my whole life, in every way for the better, even when I thought it couldn't. You are my fresh air and my open sky, you are..." he should have come up with a few more descriptions before he started, Toren realized. "...wonderful," he ended lamely. "I can't imagine living without you at my side. Carina...Carina, will you marry me?"

She was quiet for a moment, then said lightly, "Isn't it a little late to ask, after the big engagement party?"

Toren looked up and thought the smile dancing on her mouth looked tentative.

"I should have asked before," he said. "Every day I should ask you."

There were tears welling in her hazel eyes, threatening to spill over, and to Toren's horror, they didn't look like the joyous tears he had been prepared for. "What is it? What's wrong?"

One of the tears escaped down her cheek. "It's... it's...just..."

Make this right, his dragon begged.

Toren clung to her hands, desperate to fix whatever was causing her pain. "Tell me!"

"None of this is real," Carina whispered.

Toren blinked at her.

"This is just a fantasy," she said achingly. "It's just a magical compulsion, a thing you're forced to feel, because Alaska needed a queen, and your precious Compact thought I was the best choice, somehow."

"Well, you are the best choice," Toren said slowly. "But that's not how the spell works."

She slipped one of her hands away from him and dashed another stray tear from her cheek, wincing as the fresh cut flexed at her motion. "You said...it was a magical spell, a fate you couldn't escape."

Toren recaptured her hand, finally understanding. "The Compact doesn't *force* me to feel anything," he said. "I wasn't coerced into loving you, I was only allowed to see that I *could*, and oh, Carina, I did. You are so beautiful and so strong, and so smart, and so good, and Carina, I love you."

He squeezed her hand and shook his head. "I thought Raval had explained. It was a spell that made me *recognize* you, but it's gone now. No spells last, remember? Everything I feel now, everything you feel, that's *us*. That's *real*. I love you with my whole heart, not just my body, not just my dragon, not just a window to what might be, but now, entirely, with everything that I am, and that is not something that magic can even *do*."

There was hope behind the tears, hot and helpless as her eyes overflowed and Toren rose to catch her up into his arms and hold her close while she cried in relief into his arms. "Have you been feeling this *long?*" he begged. "The spell let me feel your emotions for a while, so that I would know you, and I've had to guess lately...I know you've had so much happening...we should have talked about it sooner..."

"I'm so stupid," Carina laughed and sobbed. "I couldn't feel what you were feeling anymore, either, but it never occurred to me that it was because the spell had *faded*. The *attraction* never diminished."

"Well," Toren teased, kissing her head, "I'm really hot. Everyone on my fan page says so. So of course you're going to keep wanting me. Who knows why I'm still attracted to *you*. One of life's mysteries, clearly." His playful leer belied his words.

Carina tickled him roughly, and kissed him, and they wrestled and laughed until they were wrapped up together and lying sideways across the bed.

"I have a theory," Toren said cautiously as he caught his breath. "I'm not a caster like Raval, and I don't understand the Compact like Rian, but when I looked at you, it was like I saw what could be, what was possible, like a little glimpse of the future. *This* future. When I first saw you, I saw how I feel about you *now*. Magic gave us a little head start, but it couldn't make me feel this. I love you with all of *myself*. For all of *yourself*."

"Oh, Toren," she said into his shoulder. "I love you, and I will always love you, and yes, I will marry you even if it means I have to be a queen and wear a fifty pound crown and terrible shoes…"

Then he was kissing her and she couldn't say anything else until considerably later.

EPILOGUE

*C*arina unclipped the travel buckle and started to push up the pop-up top, hissing as her shoulder reminded her that it hadn't been that long since she'd been held hostage and slashed with a magic dragon-killing dagger.

"Let me get that," Toren said, stepping in behind her to take the bar and push it in place as he stood.

It was nice, she decided, having someone to help with the camping setup and chores. More than that, it was nice having a companion, a partner. Since he was standing with his arms on either side of her anyway, it was completely natural to turn and let him kiss her.

It was *particularly* nice having someone that set her body on fire with just a glance, and Carina looked forward to showing him how the bench seat lay out into a full-sized bed.

"You want to go make the fire?" she teased him.

"That depends," Toren said archly. "Can I light it my way?"

"Can you keep the fire safely in the fire pit?" Carina asked. "Because I don't want any visits from a nosy park ranger, and it would look pretty bad for the next queen of Alaska to burn down a forest."

"I'll have you know that I have very excellent fire control," Toren said, trailing a finger down her unharmed collarbone and following it with a kiss.

"I brought marshmallows this time," Carina said with an involuntary hiss. "And the macaroni and cheese with the squeeze packet. Do you want canned ham in it or chicken?"

Toren kissed her, deeply, and while she was still trying to get her breath back, suggested, "What if you show me where the bed is in this thing, instead."

"Duty first," Carina said reluctantly. "We've got to turn on the propane for the fridge and heater and set up camp before it gets dark."

Toren groaned. "I thought we were running away from 'duty first,'" he said plaintively.

"Only for a little while," Carina comforted him. "Did you really tell them we were going to be honeymooning in Costa Rica?"

"I don't think they believed me," Toren said. "Rian saw us driving off with the van, and Fask also observed that it wasn't standard to have a honeymoon before a wedding."

"Well, we had an engagement party before the proposal, so that seems to be our general theme," Carina said as she adjusted the controls on the tiny fridge. "Besides, we're rapidly running out of days before winter, so it was now or never."

The trees outside of the van were completely bare now, and the frost was persistent in the shadows. Clouds along the horizon teased at the idea of snow.

The van was parked near the edge of a bluff, overlooking the majestic mountain range to the south, faded blue in the distance as the sky above lost its color and the horizon took on hues of pink and orange.

It threatened to be a bitterly cold night, but Carina knew she wouldn't be chilled next to Toren's heat under the quilts they'd stolen from Mrs. James' linen closets. She was wearing her new parka, and the mittens in her pockets warmed her hands whenever they grew cold.

Toren heaved a great sigh and went to dump logs haphazardly into the firepit and shift to light them on vigorous fire.

"One of these days, I'm going to show you how to make kindling and build an actual fire," Carina told him, placing the grate over some rocks and starting the water. "Come help me hang up a tarp."

Toren turned out to be as hopeless at tying knots as he was at non-magical fire management, but he was excellent at standing and holding the far corners of the tarp while Carina guyed out the ropes. "I'll teach you all these tricks," she teased him. "But you have to promise to teach me to skate and play hockey."

"I thought the Queen of Alaska didn't negotiate," Toren mocked her.

"I don't negotiate with *criminals*," Carina corrected. "Are you a criminal?"

Toren smiled foolishly at her. "I stole America's greatest treasure for myself," he said with a shrug.

While the water heated, they sat close together near the fire—in fancy new camp chairs—and watched the last of the sun's rays disappear below the horizon. The sky above darkened and began to sparkle with stars.

"I kind of miss Shadow," Toren said. "I mean, as a dog. Have you thought about getting one? A real dog, I mean?"

"I've been thinking about a *cat*," Carina confessed. "I knew a guy in Oregon who went camping with a cat, and I could be on board with that."

"The squirrels might object," Toren chuckled. "Phoebe should be having her litter soon, we can pretty much guarantee a puppy of hers isn't an evil shifter sent to murder you."

"Will Mrs. James let me have a puppy inside?" Carina asked, sorely tempted.

"I'll make her," Toren promised.

"Oh, look!" Carina said, pointing. "Northern lights! Is that one of your brothers spying on us?"

"Let them," Toren said carelessly. He had one of Carina's hands in his. "Have we had enough duty now?" he asked wistfully.

Carina nearly tipped over her camp chair climbing into his lap. "I think it's your royal duty to take me into that van and make sure that your queen doesn't get cold."

Toren stood easily with her in his arms, making her squeak in alarm. "That's my favorite duty," he said with a laugh.

And he performed it *perfectly*.

* * *

IF YOU DON'T WANT to miss book two of *Royal Dragons of Alaska*, sign up for my mailing list here and read on for more information about my other pen names and a sneak preview of The Dragon Prince's Librarian. And if you liked *The Dragon Prince of Alaska*, you'll love Shifting Sands Resort...

A NOTE FROM ELVA BIRCH

Thank you so much for picking up my book! I hope you enjoyed the story of Carina and Toren. I am looking forward to writing about his brothers, and exploring this world further.

Your reviews are very much appreciated; I read them all and they help other readers decide whether or not to buy my books!

A huge thank you to all of my fabulous beta readers and copy editors; any errors that remain are entirely my own. If you find typos or continuity problems—or you'd just like share your thoughts with me!—please feel free to email me at elvaherself@elvabirch.com. My cover was designed by Ellen Million.

To find out about my new releases, you can follow me on Amazon, subscribe to my newsletter, or like me on Facebook. Join my Reader's Retreat on Facebook for sneak previews and cut scenes! Find all the links at my webpage: elvabirch.com

I also write under other pen names—keep reading for information about my other available titles...

WRITING AS ELVA BIRCH

A Day Care for Shifters: A hot new full-length series about adorable shifter kids and their struggling single parents in a town full of mystery and surprise. Start the series with Wolf's Instinct, when Addison comes to Nickel City to take a job at a very special day care and finds a family to belong to. Funny and full of feeling, this is a gentle ice-cream-straight-from-the-container escape. Sweet and sizzling!

* * *

The Royal Dragons of Alaska: A fascinating alternate world where Alaska is ruled by secret dragon shifters. Adventure, romance, and humor! Reluctant royalty, relentless enemies…dogs, camping, and magic! Start with The Dragon Prince of Alaska.

* * *

Suddenly Shifters: A hilarious series of novellas, serials, and shorts set in the small town of Anders Canyon, where something (in the water?) is making ordinary citizens turn into shifters. Start with Something in the Water! Also available in audio!

* * *

Lawn Ornament Shifters: The series that was only supposed to be a joke, this is a collection of short, ridiculous romances featuring unusual shifters, myths, and magic. Cross-your-legs funny and full of heart! Start with The Flamingo's Fated Mate!

* * *

Birch Hearts: An enchanting collection of short stories and novellas. Unconstrained by theme or setting, each short read has romance, magic, and heart, with a satisfying conclusion. And always, the impossible and irresistible. Start with a sampler plate in Prompted 2 for fourteen pieces of sweet-to-sizzling flash fiction, or the novella, Better Half. Breakup is a free story!

WRITING AS ZOE CHANT

Shifting Sands Resort: A complete ten-book series - plus two collections of shorts. This is a thrilling shifter romance set at a tropical island resort. Each book stands alone but connects into a great mystery with a thrilling conclusion. Start with Tropical Tiger Spy or dive in to the Omnibus edition, with all of the novels, short stories, and novellas in my preferred reading order!

* * *

Fae Shifter Knights: A complete four-book fantasy portal romp, with cute pets and swoon-worthy knights stuck in a world of wonders like refrigerators and ham sandwiches. Start with Dragon of Glass!

* * *

Green Valley Shifters: A sweet, small town series with single dads, secret shifters, sweet kids, and spinsters. Low-peril and steamy! Standalone books where you can revisit your favorite characters - this series is also complete! Start with Dancing Barefoot!

* * *

Also by Zoe Chant (but not Elva Birch): **Virtue Shifters**: Sexy and funny, each book set in the little town of Virtue promises a heartwarming story, a touch of fate, and a little bit of adventure. Start with Timber Wolf!

A SNEAK PREVIEW OF THE DRAGON PRINCE'S LIBRARIAN

His first email was short, and completely professional.

> *To: t.perez@floridaulibrary.edu*
> *From: northernbookwyrm@alaska.sk*
> *Subj: Thesis topic*
> *For the attention of Ms. Tania Perez,*
> *I received your contact information from the University of Florida, Orlando, and have several questions regarding the topic of your thesis regarding the Small Kingdoms Compact and its symbolic shift. Please contact me at your convenience. I am including my direct phone number if you would prefer that method of correspondence.*
>
> *Thank you for your time,*
> *Rian*

Rian, Tania noted. A pretentious mis-spelling of a common name, or a classical Irish name? She was going to guess pretentious.

Her first email was curt, and she could not quite keep her bitterness from it.

To: northernbookwyrm@alaska.sk
From: t.perez@floridaulibrary.edu
Subj: Re: Thesis topic

*A correspondence: A **written** or **digital** communication exchanged by two parties. I would prefer to continue any contact via email and do not share my direct phone number.*

Also, you should be advised that the thesis is not currently in progress and I no longer have a copy of it, nor of the source material.

I am only a circulation librarian; you would be better served by contacting a Compact scholar with active research work.

Sincerelui,
Tania Perez

She didn't offer to point him towards such a scholar, deleted his email as soon as she replied, and expected to hear nothing more.

To her surprise, he replied with a graphic in Tolkien's Elvish that translated to *gratitude*. It would have been more sensible to assume her valediction was French than Elvish and Tania felt her ire thaw a bit even before she read the rest.

The email continued:

I appreciate your reply and your candor. I have a particular interest in your theories regarding mates and diplomatic bonds and have also seen the same obscure version of the Compact that you originally referenced.

Tania actually closed the email at that point, stood up,

and shelved books until she could bear to return to the circulation desk to read the rest of the message.

It had been almost a year since her thesis had vanished.

It wasn't just a single missing file or a random computer error. The hard copies she had printed were stolen out of her apartment while she was out, along with her copy of the old Compact, and her notes. There was no sign of a break-in—her front door was still locked! It was just seamlessly, completely, all gone. She hadn't even been able to call the police, because she had no idea how to explain that only very specific, *valueless* paperwork had gone missing, and files on a computer with a lock code had been carefully deleted.

It was like ninjas had taken it.

She'd gone to her advisor, and gotten very cagey answers about a crashed computer; for some reason, none of the drafts that she'd sent him could be found, in email or in his personal files. He claimed he would search for the hardcopy drafts, then simply never returned to the University after the holiday break; Tania returned from the hiatus to find his office empty and a flailing graduate student struggling to cover his classes.

Tania went to the dean of the college and quarreled with his secretary, who claimed that Tania didn't even have a prospectus filed with the history department. Her student ID was in the database, but her topic was *undeclared*.

Undeclared.

She'd spent her entire undergraduate career sure of what she was going to write, compiling notes, trying to find an advisor who would be a good match for the paper she wanted to work on. She had worked for nearly a year (going through four advisors) to get her premise and outline approved.

She tried to find anyone who remembered her, or her paper, but found only blank stares and head shakes; she was one student among thousands, another unremarkable face that they barely recalled. A few vaguely remembered the topic she'd been interested in, but not enough particulars to be useful.

She staggered through her classes, but couldn't maintain both the course load and the fight to find a new advisor and declare a new topic, and she couldn't simply redo her original thesis with her primary source document mysteriously missing from the library. No other school or research library seemed to have a copy, or even knew what she was referring to. At the end of the semester, struggling with her health, she was informed that her grades were not sufficient to keep her scholarship, and she still had *undeclared* for her thesis. If she could not pay, she could not continue as a student...and if she could not continue as a student, she was no longer eligible for her part-time library job after the summer break. The library director, not wanting to lose her, offered her full-time work for the fall, when their leniency would expire. With nothing else to do, and a desperate need for the health insurance that came with it, she accepted the job.

It was a surreal year, and Tania spent most of it questioning her own sanity.

But Rian...Rian *believed* her. Rian *knew* about the original Compact. Maybe she *wasn't* crazy.

It was with shaking hands that Tania logged back into her email and read the rest.

He casually mentioned the curious *dragons* reference that had gotten her side-eyed by respectable researchers, and asked about her interpretation of the *mate* language.

Tania put her head in her hands and was not sure if she laughed or cried, only knew that she was a tumble of crazy emotion.

Then she sat down and wrote back, in great detail, answering his questions and offering her own in return.

It wasn't long before he replied, and they exchanged a flurry of emailed letters, each longer than the last, as they dug into the language that she remembered, and her theories about the stranger points.

It all makes sense, she wrote, *if you keep in mind that the dragons referenced are a metaphor for the royal families. The 'protector of the lands' stuff falls into place. Possibly, the fire is an analogy for a weapon or a defensive force. I mean, I suppose it's possible they actually were dragons at the time of the Old Compact. That would explain a lot! Hahahaha.*

When he did not consider her ideas too outlandish to bear, she even, very hesitantly, with a winking emoji, suggested that the formality of the language had the kind of specificity of a ritual, or a magic spell.

His email in response treated the idea with grave consideration, and he offered a few ideas in return that made Tania long for the copy she'd had. There were so many things she would have liked to go back and double-check.

Their emails devolved into stories about their jobs, about the food they were eating, and most of all, about the books they were reading.

Some days, the letters were the only thing hauling her out of her bed, and she would check for his messages first thing, replying while she ate breakfast and decided how much she could do that day. The red flag announcing new mail became an object of joy, and she found herself lurking at her inbox at every opportunity.

They became the glowing high point of Tania's life...until she feared she was developing an unhealthy crush on someone she didn't even know, and decided to search for Rian's real identity.

The email address was her first clue. She assumed, from the address, and his mention of a uniform, that he was in some kind of security, so she went looking for more about an event he'd disparaged.

I have been to these parties, Rian told her. *It's like they read books to hate them.*

That led her to sites that she didn't usually visit, gossipy royal news sources that specialized in paparazzi photos. She was looking at the staff in the background when one of the captions caught her eye.

Twin brothers Prianriakist and Grantraykist attended the event...

Prianriakist. Prian. *Rian.*

Tania had to chuckle and lean her forehead onto her hand. Rian wasn't a pretentious mis-spelling, it was his *casual* name.

She read back through every email he'd ever sent her, and felt supremely stupid.

Of course he was a prince: the cultured tone of his writing, the oblique references to high-brow parties. His intimate knowledge of the Compact and other legal treaties.

In retrospect, it had been completely obvious.

He was a prince.

And she *wasn't* a princess.

* * *

To: t.perez@floridaulibrary.edu
  From: northernbookwyrm@alaska.sk
  Subj: Hello?

Tania,
  I don't want to be that guy, but it's been a week since you wrote back, and I'm getting worried. I got the book you recommended, and you're right, he's a blow-hard. I was

hoping to get your opinion on the chapter talking about succession.

And...I miss you. I've missed your letters this week, and I don't want to seem like a stalker, but it's not like you not to write back. I hope you're okay.

Yours, Rian

* * *

To: t.perez@floridaulibrary.edu
 From: northernbookwyrm@alaska.sk
 Subj: Re: Hello?

Dearest Tania,

Please let me know that you're alright and I haven't made you angry. If I said, or did anything, let me know and tell me how to make it right. I haven't heard from you in ten days, and I'm worried for you.

Yours always,
 Rian

To: northernbookwyrm@alaska.sk
 From: Mailer-daemon@floridaulibrary.edu
 Subj: Mail System Error, Re: Hello?

This message was undeliverable, recipient unknown. Please contact a system administrator if you believe this is in error.

Continue the story in The Dragon Prince's Librarian!

SUPPORT ME ON PATREON

What is Patreon?

Patreon is a site where readers and fans can support creators with monthly subscriptions.

At my Patreon, I have tiers with early rough drafts of my books, flash fiction, coloring pages, signed and sketched paperbacks, exclusive swag, original artwork, photographs…and so much more! Every month is a little different, and there is a price for every budget. Patreon allows me to do projects that aren't very commercial and makes my income stream a little less unpredictable. It also gives me a place to connect with my fans!

Come find out what's going on behind the scenes and keep me creating at Patreon! patreon.com/ellenmillion

Printed in Great Britain
by Amazon